WHO IS THE MIGHTY KAI?

Rise of the Djinn

Who is The Mighty Kai?
Rise of the Djinn

KENNON D OLISON SR

Ameilee Sullivan – Illustrator
Gabrielle Orris - Editor

Omni-eye Entertainment LLC

Dedicated to my Baby Girl,
Desirey C. Olison
Thank you for never giving up on me.

ACKNOWLEDGMENTS

To God the Father, and his dear son Jesus the Christ. All glory and praise to your high and Holy name. You have blessed me and kept me when no one else could.

Special thank you to Tricia Ruttman. You are the first teacher to read our story to students. You have supported me from day one. Thank you.

Special thank you to Jaime Johnson, the first 5th grader to read book 1 (Who is The Mighty Kai?). You gave me amazing feedback and ideas for the story in this book.

Special thank you to librarian Ms. Kelli Bond, the school principal, and administration for allowing me to read to the 5th graders at Gainesville Intermediate School.

Thank you to the students in Gainesville ISD for your awesome feedback and support. YOU GUYS ROCK! Especially Calvin, Ella, and Quinn.

Thank you to Mrs. LaCreasha Stille for your support throughout the school district and community.

Finally, thank you to the parents who either read the book, or encouraged their children to read and share the story. Especially Mrs. Jennifer Martin, Mrs. Jill Linnell, Mr. Quinton Jones, and Ms. Traci Beach. You are all AMAZING!

First published by Omni-eye Entertainment LLC
Gainesville, Texas. USA

Omni-eye Entertainment™
Email: info@omnieyeentertainment.com

First Edition 2023
ISBN: 979-8-218-12525-7 (Softcover)
ISBN: 979-8-218-12526-4 (Ebook)

Library of Congress Control Number: Pending
http://www.omnieyeentertainment.com
http://www.whoisthemightykai.com

Fiction: Title: Who is the Mighty Kai?: Rise of the Djinn

First Printing, 2023 by ingramspark™
http://www.ingramspark.com
Printed in the United States of America.

All illustrations, including company logos and cover art were designed by Ameilee Sullivan.

The book was professionally edited by Gabrielle Orris.

CONTENTS

Prologue

Kuwait international airport. Thursday, July 1st, 2049, CE. 9:00 a.m. local time.

Yusef Ahmed strolls casually through the airport, fully dressed in his security uniform. His face is smooth and brown, with clear skin. He is clean-shaven except for a neatly trimmed mustache. Most of his hair fits under his company-issued beret. A black briefcase with an electronic lock is cuffed to his wrist.

Yusef stops in the most crowded part of the airport. People have formed several lines to pass through the security checkpoint. There are so many people that it is hard to tell where one line begins and another ends. Yusef pushes his way to the center of the crowd, bends down, sets the briefcase on the floor, and opens it. People begin watching him because his behavior is unusual. A cool white mist seeps from the case, showing how cold its contents are.

The case contains only five small glass bottles. The clear liquid inside the bottles looks like water. Yusef calmly twists the tops from each bottle. He leaves them open in the case on the floor and stands up. He then takes his gun, points it at his temple, and blows his brains out. Blood, brains, and pieces of his skull splatter on people in the crowd as screams erupt.

Heathrow international airport, London, England. Thursday, July 1st, 2049, CE. 7:00 a.m. local time.

Six-feet-eight-inch-tall Khaled Bader calmly walks through the airport carrying a briefcase identical to Yusef's. Khaled wears a navy-blue suit, a white shirt, and no tie. He has a thin black beard to match his bushy hair. His eyes are hazel green, making him strikingly handsome.

Khaled walks to the center of a large crowd of people. He opens his briefcase and twists the tops of the five bottles; then he pulls a dagger from his breast pocket. The blade glows because it's CrimCrystal. He takes the weapon and stabs himself in the gut violently. Lime green smoke begins to disperse from his mouth, eyes, and stab wound. He trembles with pain as his body has an allergic reaction to the CrimCrystal. Then he suddenly bursts into a puff of smoke and vanishes.

| 1 |

(MC1) Mers-Cov1

Georgetown University, Washington DC, USA. Thursday, July 1st, 2049, CE. 4:00 a.m. local time.

Karen's cell phone wakes her up. Groggy-eyed, she looks at her smart device to see the time. It's 4:00 a.m. *This better be important*, she thinks to herself. She rolls over in her king-size bed, slipping a little on the satin sheets, and reaches for her phone.

"Hello?" she answers. The words barely escape her sleepy lips.

"Karen? National Press Secretary Ed Brown here." He talks fast, like it is an emergency, but he always sounds like this. "I just sent a blood sample over to your lab. I need you to hurry over there and look at it."

"I'm sorry…what?" Karen is still half asleep and unable to focus.

"Karen!" he says even more urgently. "I need you to listen to me! Wake up, Karen, wake up!"

"Ok, ok, I'm awake," Karen lies.

"Get over to your lab and check out that blood sample," he repeats.

"I don't understand," she says. "Whose blood? And why am I checking it?"

"You need to look for any viruses in that blood. The rest is classified. Call me the moment you have something. Understand?"

Just before Karen hangs up, Ed Brown says, "Oh, and Karen, this is a highly contagious and deadly virus, so you make sure and take every safety precaution."

One hour and forty-five minutes later, Karen sits on a stool looking through a microscope at the blood. She is unhappy because her perfectly arranged hair and smooth brown skin are stuffed into a biohazard suit. *Oh well,* she thinks, *the sooner I get this over with, the sooner I can take this thing off.*

Karen watches intently through the microscope as she adds a sample of healthy blood to the infected blood. The bad cells begin to attack the good cells. Within seconds the healthy cells are destroyed. Her heart sinks deep into her chest as she watches. Horror slowly creeps over her entire body as she realizes what's happening. "Oh no," she mumbles. With her heart racing, Karen pulls off her hood, picks up her cell phone, and calls the White House.

In the Oval Office of the White House Ed Brown hears his cell phone buzz. He looks down, sees the name Karen Jackson on the caller ID, and swiftly answers. "Karen? What have you found?"

"Shut down everything immediately!" she says with urgency. She talks fast, just like he usually does.

"Do you mean in the city?" he asks.

"In the world!" Karen exclaims. "Shut it all down. Transportation, government, businesses—everything!"

Ed Brown is a six-foot older man. He's American but looks like he was born in Israel. His hair is salt and pepper, but more salt than pepper. It is combed straight back away from his face and cut short. A thick mustache covers his lip that matches his hair in color. Wide-brimmed black glasses are over his eyes. He hears the panic in Karen's voice and responds immediately. "Karen, calm down. Let's not make any rash decisions just yet. We have scientists at the CDC examining this too. Let's wait for their results."

"Mr. Secretary, we may already be too late. You need to let the world know that we're on quarantine effective at once!" Karen can barely maintain her composure as she warns him.

"I don't understand. What has you so spooked?" he asks.

"Mr. Secretary, this is the Mers-Cov1 virus. It is one hundred times more deadly than Covid-19. If we don't act now, then there will be a deadly worldwide pandemic that will make 2020 look like it was a common cold, so shut it all down now! And get somewhere safe as soon as possible." Karen hangs up the phone with a worried look on her face. *What are we going to do?* she thinks. She picks up her phone and dials a new number.

"Hello, Sharon?"

| 2 |

Terror on the Train

Looked for, he cannot be seen...

Just outside of Washington DC, USA. Thursday, July 1st, 2049, CE. 6:05 a.m. local time.

"Hello?" Sharon answers her phone.

"Sharon, where are you?" Karen asks.

"We're on the train headed back to DC. After everything I went through the past few weeks, Lisa thought it would be good to get away, so we've been in New York City for a couple of days," Sharon explains.

The train begins to pick up speed. Sharon pulls her long blonde hair behind one ear and turns to look out the window. She notices that the train is passing by the trees much faster now.

"That's odd," says Lisa as she looks out the window. She's sitting next to Sharon. Her long dark brown hair is a little longer than usual. She wears her favorite army camouflage pants, a white blouse, and a green beret. She feels pretty good, aside from a few bruises she still has from her fight with Semaj.

Sharon turns forward, crosses her legs in fitted jeans, and continues her conversation. "Why? Wassup?"

"I'm gonna go check on the conductor and find out why the train is moving so fast," Lisa says as she gets up. As she walks down the aisle of the train, she notices the concerned faces of the other passengers.

"Listen," Karen explains, "there will be an announcement shortly, but I wanted to call and give you a heads up. A virus has been released. Sharon, it's deadly. It would be best to put a covering on your face right now then get off that train at the next station and go somewhere where there aren't many people."

"A virus? You mean like Covid-19?" Sharon asks.

"Yes," Karen replies, "but if you catch this one, you die. Sharon, hurry! The White House will give the announcement sometime today."

"Okay, I'll get off at the next stop. Don't worry, me and Lisa will be somewhere safe before the announcement. The stop is coming up right now."

The train comes to the station at full speed. It shows no signs of slowing down. A moment later, it rushes through the station without stopping.

"OMG!" Sharon exclaims. "Karen, I gotta go. Something's wrong. The train didn't stop, and it's picking up speed." She hangs up and immediately notices that the other passengers are panicking. Some are trying to open the doors and windows to get off the train. Then, a sword crashes through the top of the train and begins to cut a circle. People scream!

"Not again!" Sharon exclaims as a circular chunk of the ceiling falls to the floor with a loud clang. "We have *got* to stop meeting like this. People are going to start talking," she says to the hole in the ceiling.

"IT'S THAT MIGHTY KAI PERSON!" someone at the far end of the train car screams.

A different person yells, "EVERYONE GET DOWN!"

Some people scream, while others shoot their guns at the hole in the ceiling. Sharon stands there and rolls her eyes. She knows they'll never hit Kai, no matter how many bullets they shoot. Smoke bombs drop through the hole, and the train fills with dark smoke.

A man yells, "We can't see anything. Stop shooting before you hit an innocent person!"

In the darkness, Sharon feels powerfully strong arms wrap around her thin waist. The arms pull her tight until she finds herself face-to-face with Kai.

"Can I ride in just one vehicle without you cutting a hole in its roof?" Sharon asks sarcastically.

"I'm saving you." Kai's voice is metallic and electronically synthesized.

"From what?" Sharon asks as Kai lifts her through the hole. They swing from a rope that looks invisible because it reflects sunlight. Kai calls this rope '*Toranado*'. Finally, they land on a grassy area next to the train tracks as the train zooms away.

"From that!" Kai says as he points at the speeding train. Sharon looks and notices the train is about to cross a bridge over a river.

"Let go of me, please," Sharon says as she tries to break free of Kai's arms.

"What's wrong, getting a bit excited?" Kai suggests. There's a smirk under his mask.

"You need a breath corrector," she says as she pushes on his chest to put space between them. Kai winces for a split second in pain. His chest is still sore from his fight with Ominous.

"Gum?" Kai asks.

"I was thinking more like toilet paper."

"Ouch!" Kai replies.

"Don't you have a train to catch?"

Kai runs at full speed towards the river. He leaps into the air and dives. In mid-dive, he pulls *Toranado* from his forearm armor and flings it. It extends into an invisible rope and locks onto the bottom of the bridge. Kai hangs on tight and swings from the rope. He looks like he is flying instead of swinging because the rope is invisible. In mid-swing, with his body extended at a forty-five-degree angle, Kai feels his toes skim the river's water. Then he ascends towards the other side, landing twenty yards behind the train.

With blurring speed, Kai runs, then jumps and lands on a tree trunk for a split second, then catapults himself onto the train's caboose. Quickly he climbs to the top of it and runs towards the front.

Kai stops at the edge of the caboose. Moving so fast he can barely be seen; he jumps between the caboose and the train car in front of it. Then in one mighty swing, he uses his sword to cut through the metal and wires linking the two cars. Sparks fly when the cables are cut. The caboose slows down, ensuring the safety of its passengers. The rest of the train goes full speed ahead and leaves the caboose behind.

Still moving quickly, Kai reaches the gap between the next two train cars. Again, he severs them with a single mighty swing of his sword, and soon another car is freed. In mere seconds he releases the train's passenger cars one by one. Finally, he lands on the train's engine, with all the passenger cars removed.

The side window is open on the engine, so Kai sheathes his sword and quickly goes through it. He finds the conductor dead on the floor, with blood trickling from his mouth, nose, and eyes. *He died of MC1, no doubt,* Kai thinks to himself. Looking out the front window, Kai sees that the train is about to crash into the main train station at the end of the track. Undoubtedly, many in the building will be hurt if he can't stop the train.

First, he shuts down the engines. The train doesn't even slow down. Next, he applies the breaks. The wheels begin to screech and scream as they struggle to stop the speeding train. Realizing he will have to do more to stop it, he goes out the back door of the engine car. Grabbing hold of the railing on the back, Kai jumps to the ground. He tries to stop the engine by pulling it backward and planting his feet on the ground, acting like a human brake, but it keeps going and gets closer to the wall of the building. Finally, he realizes that he needs more drag to stop it completely.

He pulls out his sword, and with one hand still on the railing of the engine, he plants the blade into the ground. The sword acts as an anchor and drags a groove into the ground. Kai's arms are stretching as far as they can go, with one hand on the sword and the other on the railing. Finally, it begins to slow down.

Just when Kai thinks he has everything under control, the blade of his sword snaps. Kai, hanging on to the back of the speeding engine as it zooms down the track, looks at his broken edge and shouts, "Not again!" The engine rolls right into the building and through the wall. Brick and mortar fly everywhere. Kai is hurled into the air and through the broken wall.

Inside the building, people are waiting in line to buy train tickets. Everyone is taken by surprise when the engine suddenly breaks through. Ticket sellers are caught off guard, and the train hits several of them. Some customers see the train coming, so they move out of the way in the nick of time. People scream as the train falls over to one side, sliding through the lobby and breaking through columns that hold up the ceiling. There are decorative pipes and bars in the ceiling that come crashing down on top of innocent people. Dust fills the room from falling debris. After a few moments, the train screeches to a slow stop. People are screaming and crying.

Minutes later, the sirens of emergency responders fill the air. Soon firefighters, police officers, and medical teams enter the building and start looking for survivors. There is so much dust and debris that it's hard to see clearly. However, that does not stop people from noticing that the fallen engine, still lying on its side, begins to move. Someone is trying to lift it back to its upright position. It raises a little, teeters, then lands on its wheels. Kai is still lying on his back with his legs extended when it finally settles. He pushed the engine back to its upright position with his feet. He must have been under it when it fell over.

"It's Kai!" a fireman yells. "He must have caused all of this!"

"Get him!" a policeman yells.

Quickly, the police surround the train with guns drawn. When they get to the other side of the train, Kai is gone. They look up to the ceiling, but there's no trace of him. Someone runs to the hole in the wall to see if he ran out that way. No one's there. It's as if he's vanished into thin air.

| 3 |

The Book of the Djinn

Metropolitan Police Headquarters—the Henry J. Daly Building in Washington DC, USA. Thursday, July 1st, 2049, CE. 11:01 a.m. local time.

Remy Lang rushes into a room on the northwest side of the building. The only things in the room are a wooden table and three chairs. There is a strange light hanging from the ceiling over the table. The walls are brick, but they have been painted white, and there are no windows. The only person Remy finds in the room is the chief of police, Bill Harrison.

"When the chief of police grants you an unauthorized interview," Chief Harrison says, "with the most dangerous criminal we have, then you show up on time, Mr. Lang." He speaks with his head tilted forward so that he can see over the top of his half glasses. He is bald on top of his dark brown head and wears his usual old-fashioned three-piece suit. Remy notices that it fits extra snugly around his pot belly today.

"I know," Remy replies, "and I'm sorry. But I had to check on Sharon. She was on that train this morning. So, you know about the train crash, right?"

"Know about it? Where do you think half the force is right now? That crash makes it easier to get you in here. Are you ready?"

"Are you sure he asked for me? I mean, I don't know this guy."

"He knows you. Now listen, please try to learn as much about Kai as possible. We're sure this guy is working for him."

"I will do what I can," Remy says as he sits at the table.

The chief pushes a button on his cell phone, and one of the brick walls in the room slowly lifts upward. Behind it is a glass wall. Behind the glass are iron bars, and behind the bars sits Mike Nicholson. He is sitting at a table with his wrists chained to it. His feet are chained to the legs of the chair, which is welded to the floor. He's wearing a city-issued orange jumpsuit. Mike is a good-looking white male with sandy brown hair cut short on the sides but long and bushy on top. He has a bushy beard to match his hair. His soft brown eyes see everything going on at once.

"What's his name?" asks Remy.

"His identification says his name is 'Mike Nicholson', but we think it's a fake," replies the chief. "Well, there he is. The man that attacked Sharon."

"WHAT!?" Remy exclaims. "This is the same guy? He was the decoy on Copper Field, and he attacked Sharon earlier that day in Karen's lab?" Remy looks at Mike with fire in his eyes. Anger overwhelms him. "You better be glad there are bars between you and me!"

"Calm down!" Mike says with an evil smirk. "No one wants your pitiful, pathetic little girlfriend."

Remy has a brief look of relief on his face. Mike notices and doesn't like it, so he says, "But it might be fun to see how long she can scream before passing out."

In a rage, Remy picks up a chair and throws it at Mike. The chair hits the glass wall and falls to the floor without leaving a single mark on the glass. Throwing the chair took all of Remy's energy and strength. He falls to his knees, sweating, and his nose trickles with blood. Mike gives an evil smile at Remy's anger.

"I would love to sit here and taunt you all night," Mike says, "but I don't know how much time I have, and there's a lot to tell you, Remy Lang."

"Nonsense," replies the chief, "we have all the time in the world. You are not going anywhere anytime soon, my friend."

"I assure you," Mike says with a new smirk, "when the Djinn realize where I am, they will come. Remy," he continues, "you are the only one I know who can reach Kai."

The chief looks at Remy with suspicion. Remy looks back with a puzzled look, then he leans into the chief's ear and says, "I don't know what he's talking about. But play along so we can get the information out of him." Chief Harrison nods for the moment, but later, he will check out the connections between Remy and Kai.

"Why do you need me to reach Kai?" Remy asks.

"I'm a YellowJacket. We're half-breeds," answers Mike. "My great-grandfather was a Djinn, but his wife, my great-grandmother, was not. Being a half-breed made it easy for me to fool the Djinn into thinking

I'm one of them. Since they accept me as one of their own, they include me in their secret plans. I take that information and report back to the YellowJackets. Our goal is to stop the Djinn. We believe that Kai is the only person who can do that."

"Is that why you dressed up like Kai?" asks Remy.

"Yes," answers Mike. "We needed him to take down Ominous. My job was to draw the police away so Ominous and Kai could settle their differences."

"You want Kai to destroy these so-called Djinn so that the YellowJackets can take the Djinn's place, right?" asks the chief.

"Right," answers Mike.

"Oh, so you believe in Djinn and YellowJackets?" asks Remy.

"I don't know who these Djinn are," answers the chief, "but we know the YellowJackets. They're a good old-fashioned street gang. We know about five of you. Well, counting you, there are six. How many more of you are there?"

Mike doesn't answer, so the chief presses a button on his phone, which turns on the strange light hanging over the table. It's a hologram projector. Five holograms of different people now hover over the table. Each person looks very different from the others except for one thing: they all wear striking yellow leather jackets. The jackets have black trim down the front on both sides of the zipper. The trim flairs out and up towards the shoulders, making it look like the letter Y.

The chief reaches out and touches the hologram of Amber Rains. His touch makes her hologram grow larger and move into the center of the others. The other holograms get smaller and slowly circle above Amber. "Who is she?" he asks.

"Amber Rains, our leader," says Mike. "She is code-named '*Breeze*.' She can control certain types of violent weather with her mind. But once she starts it, she can't stop it."

The chief and Remy look at Amber closely. She is a white female with short brown hair and solid dark black eyes. The haircut makes her look like a boy. Her very fit figure hides in loose-fitting pants for fighting and black combat boots.

Chief Harrison touches the next hologram. It changes places with Amber's. He looks at Mike and waits for him to explain who the next person is.

"The bleach blonde with the old-fashioned cowboy hat is Mateo Diego," explains Mike. "They call him *'El Caballero'* or *'The Knight.'* His father is a Djinn who took a human wife in Spain. He has lived many, many years. We know little about him except for one thing: he is a weapons specialist. He seems to be constantly pulling out futuristic gadgets."

The chief touches the next hologram. Again, he waits for an explanation from Mike.

"El Caballero's half-brother," Mike announces. "His name is Sheppard Gonzales. He can summon the mysterious powers of the dead. We call him *'Tombstone.'* El Caballero and Tombstone have the same father. The difference is that Tombstone's human mother came from Mexico."

The Chief touches the next hologram. It's a black man who wears a black flat-brimmed hat known as a "*sombrero Cordoba*." Under it, he wears a black sackcloth mask that covers his eyes and the top of his head under his hat. His eyes are green, and the bottom half of his face is clean-shaven except for a skinny gray mustache under his nose.

"We don't know his name," says Mike. "We don't know what he looks like under that mask either. He didn't ask us to do so, but we call him *'The Challenge.'*"

"Why?" asks Remy.

"Because whenever we face an impossible task, he says, 'Challenge Accepted.'"

The chief touches the next hologram. It's an ordinary-looking woman with golden blonde hair and thick, black, horned-rimmed glasses. The glasses cover her face, from her eyebrows to her upper cheekbone. She wears an old-fashioned yellow archer hat and has a large bow strapped across her body.

"And who is this lady?" the chief asks.

"*HallowPoint*," Mike flatly says. "Her name is Sophie Turner. She's the only one of us that can match the speed of the Djinn. That bow of hers doesn't require arrows. Instead, it generates electronic energy bolts."

"There's one more YellowJacket member, isn't there?" Remy asks.

"I am '*The Instigator*,'" Mike says. "Now that you have what you want," Mike continues impatiently, "can we get down to why I asked you here, Mr. Lang?"

The chief and Remy look at each other with a look that asks, '*Should we let him speak or ask more questions?*' Then, after a moment of silence, they turn and look at Mike, giving him their full attention.

"There is a book that you need to give Kai," Mike explains.

"That's Sharon's book," Remy says.

"No, not her book. Sharon's book is unreliable," Mike states flatly. "Tell me, Mr. Lang, have you seen a Djinn yet?"

"I'm not sure. I think so," Remy answers.

"Do you think you should warn others about them? Could your experience with them help others?" asks Mike.

"Of course," answers Remy.

"That book, the one your crybaby girlfriend had, is called '*The Ancient Djinn,*'" Mike continues. "Over thousands of years, people recorded their encounters with Djinn in that book. They did it to help other people learn how to survive them."

"We need that book! Where is it?" demands Remy.

"Beware of that book. So many things in it are untrue. But there is another book," Mike explains.

"Another book?" asks Remy.

"It's called '*The Book of the Djinn,*' and the Djinn themselves wrote it. That book contains all their secrets," Mike says.

"Where are these books?" asks the chief.

"The '*Ancient Djinn*' is well hidden. I need it for leverage when they come to get me. But the '*Book of the Djinn,*' I saw last with Dr. Stephen Powers. He will know where it is now," Mike concludes.

"First of all," demands the chief, "you're going to tell us where you hid that book. And I assure you, no one is coming through these steel walls to get you."

At that moment, Officer Bill Fitzpatrick rushes into the room. "Chief, you need to see this. You too, Mr. Lang," he says in his familiar Scottish accent. His voice is rushed, hurried, and urgent.

Both men follow Officer Bill into the lobby. Pastor Arthur Amsu and Pastor Arze Seth are the only people in the hall. They are co-ministers for the 12th street Christian church in Washington, DC. Pastor Amsu pushes Pastor Seth in a wheelchair.

On the TV screen in the lobby is the signal for the Emergency Broadcast System with the familiar long, uninterrupted beep. Remy checks his phone, and the alert is also there. *It must be on every device,* Remy thinks to himself.

Pastor Amsu says, "We're here to see if our church can assist with the train wreck. But when we came in we saw the alert on the TV screen."

The chief is about to answer him when the long beep stops, and Ed Brown, the White House press secretary, appears on the screen. It is 11:25 a.m. EST. He's standing behind a podium with a prepared written statement. When he's sure the cameras are recording, he says, "At 9:00 a.m. Kuwait time, and at 2:00 a.m. local time, a deadly virus known as Mers-Cov1, code-named MC1, was released at the Kuwait international airport. At about the same time, the virus was released at Heathrow International Airport in London, England. Unfortunately, we have no vaccine or cure for this virus. Symptoms can take up to twelve hours to appear.

"The World Health Organization is declaring a worldwide pandemic and medical emergency. All transportation, governments, and businesses are to shut down immediately. We are encouraging local cities and states to declare Marshall Law. Stay home until further notice.

"If you experience symptoms, do not go to the hospital. They can do nothing for you, and you will spread this highly contagious virus even further. This virus has a ninety percent kill rate within twenty-four hours. If you catch it, you will have only a few hours…." Ed Brown coughs up blood onto the sheet of notes he's reading from, "…to get your affairs in order." Then, horrified, he says, "Stay tuned to this channel for updates as we work to get a vaccine. May God be with us all, and may God bless America."

Everyone looks at Remy, whose nose is still bleeding a lot. He is also sweating from his forehead. "It's not what you think," he says.

"But still," the chief says, "I think you had better go on home. Everyone, go home."

At that moment, Remy grabs the back of a nearby chair to keep his balance, but the chair tilts backward and he falls to the floor, passed out. Blood trickles from his nose and mouth. The others stand around stunned, realizing they have all been infected if Remy has the virus.

| 4 |

Haptic Holograms

A Secret Underground Training Facility, Washington DC, USA. Thursday, July 1st, 2049, CE. 11:15 a.m. local time.

Sifu Sun Chang and Ms. Jennie Davis stand in a homemade wooden elevator. It has a wooden floor, no walls or ceiling, and planks for guard rails on all four sides. It hangs in an old, bottomless shaft that is dusty and filled with cobwebs. To lower the lift, you must pull on the thick rope that hangs to one side. Sifu Sun spent years repairing the ride. Now, he leans over the wooden guard rail, lowering it. Unfortunately, being only five feet seven inches tall makes it difficult for him to reach the ropes. Not to mention his big belly is in the way. Sifu Sun's long black hair, which he wears braided down his back, and full-length black beard make the elevator shaft hot. It isn't long before he's sweating.

Ms. Jeannie Davis sets her belongings on the floor and brushes her ponytail out of her face. She grabs the guard rail and hangs on tight as the rickety elevator sways and rocks a little more with each pull of the rope.

"How far down is it?" she asks.

"Exactly two thousand six hundred forty feet," he grunts as he lowers them further. "The American government had this place built over one hundred years ago."

"Why?"

"It was designed to hide the president and his men during an attack. It was a top-secret project," he can barely say the words because he's so out of breath.

"How did you know about it?"

Finally, they hit bottom. Sifu Sun takes a moment to catch his breath and then answers, "My ancestors worked on it. It's directly below my house. When I came to America, I bought this house because I knew what lies beneath it."

They walk out of the lift into a state-of-the-art martial arts training facility. The entrance looks like an airplane hangar. The main room is huge and empty except for wrestling mats on the floor and mirrors on the walls. The ceiling is at least one hundred feet high. Through the back are several hallways that lead to other rooms.

"My goodness, it's huge," says Ms. Davis. "How many square feet?"

"Ten thousand," answers Sifu Sun.

Sifu Sun Chang has secretly turned this place into a martial arts training facility over the last seven years. Unfortunately, it's less impressive than the one in Hong Kong. Back then, he was the best martial arts teacher in the country, maybe even the world.

"Why did you have to bring so much stuff?" complains Sky.

Ms. Davis looks to her left and sees two of her sons carrying a large trunk down some stairs. On one side of the chest is Playmaker, the team leader of the Shadows. On the other side is his brother, Sky.

"I like to be prepared," answers Wiz.

Wiz is dressed just like a 1930's chauffeur. His hat looks like what a cab driver would have worn back then. It has goggles wrapped around it over the front bill. He wears leather gloves that come up to his elbows. For some reason, he has tucked his pants into his knee-high boots. Last, he has on a double-breasted coat with buttons on both sides.

Extra and Tea step off the stairs, out of breath from laughing. The girls are wearing skates and carrying a little red wagon. Ms. Davis wonders how they could bring it down the stairs in skates without falling.

"That's the funniest one yet!" Extra says, laughing.

"What is he thinking?" mocks Tea.

"It's not like we don't make enough fun of him already," Extra states.

"What are you two laughing at?" asks Sky.

The girls point to Wiz.

"Do you see how he's dressed?" Tea replies.

"I can't with him," Extra giggles.

"Yea? Well, you're a nincompoop!" Wiz does his best clap back.

The girls stop laughing, look at each other, then bust out laughing even harder.

"We're a what?" laughs Extra.

"I think he just called us poop!" shouts Tea with a smile.

"Nincompoop!" Wiz corrects them. "It means idiot. Oh, never mind, why do I waste my time? Smaller brains will never get me."

"Wiz, you brought too much stuff," Playmaker explains. "We're only gonna be here for a few days."

Upon hearing Playmaker's comment, Sifu Sun turns to Ms. Davis and says, "You haven't told them?"

Ms. Davis gives a guilty smile but doesn't answer.

"We're here for six weeks for training," Sifu Sun announces.

Sky looks at the facility and says, "Six weeks here? There's NOTHING here! Aww, man. This is gonna suck!"

"But mom," Wiz whines, "how are we supposed to watch the *Magnificent Crime Fighter*? He will finally find '*The Lover*' and stop him for good this week. And we're gonna miss it!"

"'*The lover*'?" asks Ms. Davis.

"Yea, Mom, he hates violence so much that when someone does violence, he destroys them by cutting them into pieces," Wiz explains.

"We need to evaluate what you watch on tv, young man," Ms. Davis says sternly.

At that moment, Research steps off the stairs and into the room. He carries a backpack full of electronic equipment.

"What took you so long?" asks Playmaker.

"I was setting up relay agents," he answers.

"What's that?" Tea questions.

"Satellites provide internet service," Research explains, "and can only reach so far. So sometimes, we hit spots where there's no signal. That's why your texts won't go through sometimes, or your phone call drops. It's because..."

Extra walks over to him and pokes him in the forehead several times as he talks.

"Ouch!" Research says. "What the heck are you doing?"

"Looking for the 'skip intro' button, you moron. Just tell us what a relay agent is. Geez!"

"It gives us internet access way down here," Research answers.

"There's no internet service down here," Sifu Sun explains.

"Sure, there is! I set up relay agents on the stairs every one-hundred meters. Now we have a signal," explains Research.

Sifu Sun is about to explain that he does not allow internet access during training when everyone's phone starts ringing. It's an emergency broadcast. Everyone takes out their devices to see what's going on.

"What is this?" asks Wiz. "Why is my phone acting all weird?"

"It's the old Emergency Broadcast System," answers Ms. Davis. "It's how the government would announce a national emergency years ago. But I haven't seen it used in at least twenty years."

The beep periodically stops, and a voice comes through and says, "This is not a test. You are being alerted to a national emergency. Please stand by for an announcement from our government." This message repeats several times for a few minutes. At 11:25. a.m. EST, the beep stops. On the screens of everyone's devices is Ed Brown, the white house press secretary, standing at a podium with his prepared statement. When he coughs up blood onto his notes, the kids gasp. Even Ms. Davis has a horrified look on her face. Once the broadcast goes dead, the kids bombard Ms. Davis with questions.

"I don't get it. What's going on?" asks Tea.

"Yea, what did that mean?" echoes Playmaker.

"So, is everyone gonna get sick?" asks Sky.

"And die?" adds Wiz.

Sifu Sun looks at Ms. Davis and asks, "You knew about this, didn't you? That's why you rushed over and brought so many things."

"Listen, everyone," Ms. Davis says as she ignores Sifu Sun's question. "Yes, people will get sick. Yes, people will die. But we will be safe if we stay here until it's over." She looks at Research and says, "Go quickly and remove the relay agents. There can be no outside communication. No one can know we're here."

Research hurries up the stairs to remove the relay agents.

Ms. Davis turns to the other kids and says, "Does everyone understand?" All the kids nod their heads.

"But why mom?" Research asks.

"In time, things will become clear," Sifu Sun answers. "In the meantime, we will stay here until this ends."

"Aww, man! How long will that be?" asks Sky.

"You are unhappy with your new home?" asks Sifu Sun. "You seem ungrateful for the comforts of life provided for you."

"No, it's not that," answers Sky. "But I mean, look at this place. There's nothing to do here!"

"You will train," Sifu Sun assures him.

"Train with what?" asks Playmaker. "Sky is right. This place is completely empty."

Sifu Sun pulls up the sleeve on his right arm, revealing a tattoo that looks like an electronic control panel. The tattoo lights up. He pushes one of its buttons and twists it so that it turns like a dial, and the room suddenly fills with holograms. The holograms are of various equipment for martial arts training. The walls have hologram weapons, padded wooden Wing Chun dummies, and even kung fu stretchers.

"Oh great," Sky says sarcastically. "Holograms?! We can't do any real training with this stuff. We need things you can hold, hit, and fight with."

Sifu Sun turns another dial on his arm, and a single hologram of a Djinn appears in the center of the room. The Djinn is at least seven feet tall. He's nothing more than a silhouette of black. He wears a 1930s hat that looks like a Fedora. It's tilted low in the front, so his face can't easily be seen. He has a black tie, white shirt, black suit, and black trench coat that comes down to the middle of his shins. He wears black and white leather dress shoes.

"Am I supposed to be scared?" asks Sky sarcastically. "What's he supposed to be?"

"*That* is a Djinn," answers Sifu Sun. "You will train to defend yourself against them."

"You mean those Genie you told us about?" asks Tea.

"He's just a hologram," Sky says. "He can't hurt us. We need to train to fight real people. Not holograms."

"My young Sky," Sifu Sun says, "feel free to show us all how to defeat the hologram."

"Yea, Sky, square up!" Research challenges.

Sky starts walking towards the hologram Djinn. As he approaches, he says, "Guys, it's just light. It's a hologram, for crying out loud! I can just walk—"

The hologram Djinn pulls back his trench coat, revealing a half-sword. He grabs his sword and swings, striking Sky he speaks. Sky flies backward ten feet and lands on his back. The kids are cracking up.

"The unmighty Sky," Extra laughs.

Research sings, "I believe I can fly; I believe I can touch the sky...."

Even Ms. Davis has to choke back a chuckle.

"He laid the smack down on you," laughs Wiz.

"The holograms turn solid when you touch them," explains Sifu Sun. "They're called Haptic Holograms."

The kids let out various comments like "cool" and "wow".

Research says, "That's wassup!"

"You could have said that," Sky grumbles as he gets up, rubbing his side, "*before* I made a fool of myself."

"Some lessons," Sifu Sun answers, "must be experienced. So, what did you learn from this experience?"

"Not to trust you," Sky says with a frown.

"If that is what you have learned from this experience, then you will repeat it," replies Sifu Sun.

"How many times will he repeat the lesson?" asks Wiz.

"My young Wushi," Sifu Sun says, patting him on the head, "as many times as needed."

"As many times as needed for what?" Wiz questions.

"For him to learn the lesson," Sifu Sun says as he turns his attention back to his tattooed control panel.

| 5 |

You're Tall

A Secret Underground Training Facility, Washington DC, USA. Thursday, July 1st, 2049, CE. 11:43 a.m. local time.

Sifu Sun pushes another button on his tattoo control panel and the hologram of the Djinn changes to a hologram of an obstacle course. Everything on it is see-through and outlined in tints of red and green. The floor is five feet in the air, with a red hue of light that beams throughout it. Above the floor hovers a hologram of a military drone.

Sifu Sun whistles, and a shadowy hooded figure appears at the far end of the obstacle course. He wears all black, and his hood extends into a cloak that drapes over his shoulders. The bottom of the cloak stops just short of the back of his knees. The hem is jagged, as if it was torn from something when it was made. He wears a face covering, making the hood appear to be empty.

The person runs towards the obstacle course and leaps into the air. He twists and turns in mid-air and lands on the electric red floor. Immediately the drone fires a storm of laser bolts at him. The figure pulls out two swords that were crisscrossed on his back and blocks each laser bolt.

The drone shoots, trying to find an opening to hit him, but it's as if the figure knows where the bolts will hit before they land, and he blocks every one of them.

"Epic!" says Sky.

"That's wassup!" Research agrees.

All the kids watch intently as the figure battles the drone. After a moment, the floor of the hologram shifts into individual squares. It looks like the figure is standing on a transparent checkerboard. The squares begin to disappear randomly and reappear. The figure must fight the drone while hopping to a square of the floor that hasn't disappeared. He does well for only a moment, then tries to land on a square that vanishes before he can reach it. His foot falls through the floor. He drops one of his swords and gets hit with a laser bolt. The moment he's hit, the entire floor disappears, dropping him five feet.

"Whoa, that was cool!" exclaims Wiz.

"I don't have the tea on that," says Tea.

The figure pulls off his hood, revealing his identity as Drew Chang. His face is still bruised from the beating he took a few weeks ago at the hands of the Pirates. He sits up and grasps his side gingerly. As soon as the Shadows see who it is, they all run to him.

"Drew, where did you learn to do that?" asks Playmaker.

"Yea, and can you teach us?" Sky begs.

"What happened to your face?" Extra interrupts.

Everyone stares at her for being rude.

"What?" she says. "Everyone was thinking it. I was just the only one with enough guts to ask."

Drew stands up, smiles, and points to his father. "Father has been teaching me," he says.

They walk back over to Ms. Davis and Sifu Sun Chang. As they go, they continue to talk.

"If that's the face I end up with by learning from your father, then I'm good," Extra says.

Drew gives her a dirty look and says, "Don't be stupid. My father didn't do this to me."

"It was the Pirates, huh?" Tea asks.

"Of course," says Wiz. "They've been out to get you for a long time."

"They broke into our house and jumped me. That's why Father decided it's time for me to train."

"You've learned much in a short time, my son. But your failure in the obstacle course shows you have much more to learn."

"That course is impossible," states Playmaker.

"You can't be serious about putting my boys on that course," Ms. Davis says with a worried look.

"In time," Sifu Sun explains, "you must all master that course.

"It's impossible. No one can master that course," complains Research.

Sifu Sun points to the obstacle course. Everyone turns to see The Mighty Kai standing at its edge. No one heard or saw him enter the room, but there he stands just as Drew did. Kai leaps into the air and lands on the five-foot-high platform. Immediately the hologram of the military drone appears again and starts firing at Kai. Kai flips over, dodges, and ducks away from the energy bolts sent his way. But with each move, he gets closer to the drone. Finally, when he is close enough, he takes his sword and strikes the hologram, destroying it.

Immediately the floor turns into checkerboard squares, just like before, the squares flash on and off. Kai leaps effortlessly to solid squares as they appear. It's almost as if he knows where the square will turn solid before it does.

Suddenly, for no reason, Kai leaps forward into the air as if jumping through a floating ring. In mid-dive, a vortex appears, and Kai's body is halfway through it. It's as if he knew when and where the vortex would appear before it did. The vortex disappears after Kai passes through it, and Kai lands in a tuck and rolls on the flashing checker floor. As soon as he lands, he leaps into the air again. This time he misses the vortex, and the entire hologram shuts off. Kai falls to the floor, landing on his feet without a sound.

The kids stand there, in awe of what they've seen. No one makes a sound as Kai walks toward them, their mouths open, eyes wide.

Finally, Research breaks the silence. "That's fire!"

There's a pause, and then Sky yells, "Epic!"

When Kai finally reaches the kids, he stops momentarily and gives them a chance to get a good look at him.

"That has to be the coolest thing I've ever seen," says Playmaker.

"I felt that way when I first saw the obstacle course, too," Kai says, using his metallic machine-like voice to hide his identity.

"No, I mean you!" Playmaker clarifies.

Wiz stands there in his 1930's chauffeur outfit, feeling just a tiny bit embarrassed. He would have worn his *Magnificent Crimefighter* uniform if he knew he would be meeting The Mighty Kai. That would have been much more appropriate. Nonetheless, he stands there, face to thigh with Kai himself. Wiz has no idea what to say. Then, without thinking, the words, "You're tall," fall out of his mouth.

Upon hearing this, Kai looks down as if he just now noticed Wiz standing there. Then he stoops as far as he can and crouches on one knee. With his face just about level with Wiz's, he says, "But you know what? When I take my shoes off, I'm the same size as you."

Everyone laughs. Everyone, that is, except for Ms. Davis. She stands there like a fifth grader with a crush on her teacher. She hears the laughter but is mesmerized by this dangerous criminal they call Kai.

"Drew," Sifu Sun says, "take the team and show them how the haptic holograms work."

"Yes, Father." Drew leads the Shadows over to the area where the holograms were appearing. When they're far enough away, the three adults begin to talk.

"Are the Djinn responsible for this virus?" asks Sifu Sun.

"I think they are, but I don't know for sure," Kai answers as they walk towards the elevator shaft. "I can tell you this: If Djinn released this virus, there's a hidden agenda behind it. The virus isn't their main cause. They can't imprison a world if there are no people to imprison. No." Kai pauses momentarily, thinking. "There's a reason behind this virus. We just don't know what it is yet."

"Maybe there are answers in Sharon's book," Sifu Sun suggests.

"Do you have any leads on where to find it?" asks Kai.

"Not yet, but I am hoping Remy has something soon."

"I have people looking for it, too," Ms. Davis says, finally finding her voice.

"By the way, don't let Remy down here," Kai advises with concern. "He's sick. Until we know for sure that it's not this virus, it's better to be safe than sorry."

"What about Sharon and Lisa?" asks Ms. Davis.

Kai pauses for a moment. His heart sinks into his chest at the thought of Sharon being sick. Then, after another moment, he finds his words and says, "I was with her this morning. She seemed fine."

"I don't have to look under your mask to recognize true love," Sifu Sun says.

"You mean Kai and Sharon?" asks Ms. Davis. "But doesn't she like Remy?"

"What?" asks Kai in surprise. Even with his disguised, metallic voice, his jealousy comes through. There's a tense silence. No one says a word, because Kai is famous for his temper. Sifu Sun and Ms. Davis still don't know him well, and each feel that it's better to be careful not to anger him.

To change the subject, Kai says, "At a time when the streets should be empty, the YellowJackets and the Pirates have been extremely active." He enters the elevator shaft, turns, and faces Sifu Sun and Ms. Davis. "I'll patrol the streets to see what I can find. Something doesn't feel right."

"Aren't you worried about catching the virus?" Ms. Davis asks.

"No," Kai says flatly.

"We must stay here and train," Sifu Sun states. "We'll be of no help until we're prepared properly."

"What about Pathos?" asks Kai. "I'll need his help to defeat Gideon. He's much too powerful for me to fight alone."

"He'll need a mask or vaccine to protect him from the virus. Until then, he cannot help you."

"I'll take care of that for him. I need all the help I can get."

"Once we learn how to control your power, then you'll be able to defeat anyone," Sifu sun says.

Kai takes *Toranado* from under his forearm armor and throws it up the elevator. It extends into an invisible rope. Kai slowly rises by hanging on to it. It looks like Kai's floating away.

"Where are you going now?" asks Sifu Sun.

"To find out who's behind this virus and why," Kai says as he rises out of sight.

"I fear the Great War has begun," says Sifu Sun as Kai disappears up the elevator shaft. "There will be some dark days ahead."

| 6 |

The Harvest

The Smithsonian National Museum of Natural History, Washington DC. Tuesday, August 10th, 2049, CE. 9:00 a.m. local time.

Dr. Stephen Powers stands in the center of a small empty secret room. He checks his watch to ensure he's on time for his meeting with *The Three Little Ladies.* As he checks his watch, three holograms appear. The first is Utopia Berger, the second is Cartelina Oleum, and the third is Caballa Lappen. These are *The Three Little Ladies* he's been waiting for. They are the masterminds behind the Djinn's rise to power.

"Good of you to be on time, Dr. Powers," Utopia says. When she speaks, her hologram moves to the center of the room in front of Dr. Powers while the others hover above.

"Yes, ma'am," Dr. Powers replies. "Has the meeting of the world leaders started?"

"It started five minutes ago," answers Utopia. Her eyes are large and black in the center but covered in light blue eyeshadow and black eyeliner to hide her wrinkled pink skin. Her cheekbones are high and painted with bright pink rouge in a circle. Her nose is long, and her mouth is wide with bright red lipstick. She wears a white-feathered black hat on her head, and her neck is covered in a matching scarf. "They're asking the World Health Organization about a vaccine," she continues.

"We're right on time then," suggests Dr. Powers. "When we hack into their video chat, you ladies stay quiet. I don't want them to know you're there. Let me talk."

The ladies all agree. They sit quietly as Dr. Powers opens a virtual control panel that hangs in midair. It's made entirely of light. Dr. Powers pushes a few buttons and hacks into the emergency meeting. He presses a few more buttons to convert each world leader's signal into holograms. Hundreds of holograms float above him. There's one hologram below the others, centered in the room. On it is Y.R. King, the president of the United States. She has long, beautiful, wavy black hair that hangs just to her shoulders. Her eyes have a deep concern as she speaks.

Dr. Powers enters the video call while President King is speaking, "…and half my staff is dead," she says. "At this rate, I won't have an administration by the end of the month. When will a vaccine be ready?"

An older man—a doctor—replaces the president in the center of the room. His name is Salem Addisu. He has a short grey afro cut into a flat top, thick grey eyebrows, and a matching mustache. Thin horn-rimmed glasses sit on his face. Dr. Powers watches and listens as Mr. Addisu answers. "We will need at least another six months before a trusted vaccine is made available," he says.

The world leaders begin to yell and growl in protest. "We can't wait that long!" Ansel Schmidt, the chancellor of Germany, shouts.

"We will all be dead by then!" Anna Smirnov exclaims. She's the president of Russia.

Dr. Powers uses the confusion to take control of the meeting. He turns his volume as loud as possible. "SILENCE!" he says. The words are so loud that it sounds like he's screaming. "I can help all of you."

The holograms go silent. After a moment or two, Wang Wei, the president of China, speaks up. "Who are you?"

"Dr. Powers, is that you?" President King asks. "How did you get into this meeting?"

"That doesn't matter," Dr. Powers answers. "What's important is that I'm here and I can help you."

"I order you to get off this secured line and report to my office," demands President King.

"One of yours?" asks Jill Davies, the prime minister of England. She has a smirk on her face, knowing how embarrassing this is for the President.

"Yes," she answers. "I'll take care of this."

"Mute," Dr. Powers says.

Instantly, the president of the United States is muted. Everyone can see her talking, but no one hears her. When she realizes she's muted, she yells and screams even louder. Jill Davies chokes back a laugh at how silly President King looks.

"You're no longer in charge, Madame President," Dr. Powers explains. "Your days of ruling are over." He then looks at the rest of the world leaders and says, "All of your days of ruling are over."

The world leaders scream and shout in anger. But Dr. Powers waves his hand for them to be silent. "Quiet!" he calmly says. His voice booms loudly again. "Or I shall mute all of you!" They slowly follow his direction. "As I said before, I'm here to help."

"How can you help?" Prime minister Davies asks.

"I represent a company known as 'The Harvest,'" Dr. Powers explains. "We have a fully tested vaccine ready to be given now." The crowd of world leaders cheers and applauds. "But there is a price," Dr. Powers continues.

"There is always a price," President Smirnov says.

"We are willing to pay anything," Kim Kye-Chul, the North Korean supreme leader, shouts.

"I know this is hard for you to hear," Dr. Powers explains, "and even harder for you to accept. But in time, you will understand that what we're doing is better for the world. You have no choice. Each of you will surrender your country to The Harvest. In exchange, you will get your vaccines." The words cut like knives into the world leaders.

"Have you lost your mind?" an unknown voice shouts.

"Preposterous!" another leader cries.

"So basically, you'll take over the whole world, and in exchange we get to live? We'll die first!" President Smirnov shouts.

The hologram of an older man from Transylvania appears centered in the room. "My country stinks of dead bodies," he says. "We have no place to bury them. And even if we did, we have no one to bury them. My fellow citizens will be extinct soon if something is not done. We accept your demand."

"Everyone must agree," announces Dr. Powers, "or there will be no vaccines for any of you. Go back to your governments. Have your meetings, do what you must to lay down your power and save your lives."

"You will release the vaccine to us, or we will find you and take it from you," Supreme Leader Kim Kye-Chul states.

"I see I have my answer," says Dr. Powers. "I will return to this meeting on August 26th at 9:00 a.m. eastern standard time. Those of you who are still alive can return here at that time. Maybe then you'll be ready to accept our terms.

"One last thing. If there is any mention of this meeting to the public or the press, then you will never get your vaccine."

With this final statement, he hangs up the call. All the holograms instantly disappear except for *The Three Little Ladies*. When he's sure all the others are gone, Dr. Powers asks, "Okay, so what now?"

"Now," Utopia answers, "we wait. They don't realize that without our vaccine, they'll all be dead. When they do, they'll gladly give up their power."

"Pax Ordo is upon us," says Cartelina.

"And what about Kai?" asks Caballa.

"Gideon will soon have the book called '*The Ancient Djinn,*'" Utopia answers. "When Kai finds that out, he'll find Gideon, then Gideon will finally complete our King's final command and kill Kai. But There's something else," Utopia says. "When Gideon was in downtown Washington DC, the Amulet of Zahra glowed brighter than ever."

"What does that mean?" asks Cartelina.

"We are not sure," answers Utopia, "but it could be...."

"Prince Ceneric!" Caballa finishes her statement.

"We don't know for sure," Utopia explains, "but yes, we think Prince Ceneric may be buried there."

"Have the secret service agent Djinn seal off the area," Cartelina says to Dr. Powers.

"Shouldn't we wait until we control the world?" asks Dr. Powers.

"No," answers Utopia. "With the virus raging, the streets will be clear. We should be able to dig without prying eyes. Have them start digging for our prince right away. With Ceneric released, The Mighty Kai's days are surely numbered."

| 7 |

Pathos

A Secret Underground Training Facility, Washington DC, USA. Thursday, August 20th, 2049, CE. 5:52 p.m. local time.

The Shadows watch as Drew leaps through the vortexes on the obstacle course. He leaps forward into the air as if jumping through a floating ring. In mid-dive, a vortex appears, and Drew's body is halfway through it. It's as if he knows when and where the vortex will appear before it does. The vortex disappears after Drew passes through it, and he lands on the flashing checker floor. His landing only lasts a split second before he leaps into the air again. He repeats this process until he's passed through several vortexes, then everything stops. The drone hovering above buzzes, whistles, and vibrates a little.

An electronic voice that sounds a lot like Kai says, "Level 2 achieved."

Instantly, the hologram obstacle course changes to a solid, glowing lime-green floor. A hologram of a Djinn stands alone in front of Drew. The Djinn throws back one side of his coat like a gunfighter in the old west to reveal a half sword. As the Djinn draws his weapon, Drew pulls out two swords. The Djinn leaps into the air and swings his blade in a downward chopping motion at Drew's forehead. Drew blocks and the swords clang. Drew's blades are now in a parallel position, turned sideways while pressed against the sword of the Djinn. Drew crouches under the weight and force of the Djinn as he presses downward to try and break Drew's block. Drew falls to one knee before the Djinn takes a step back.

At that moment, Drew stands back up. He shuffles his feet and shifts his balance. His shuffle does nothing to help him win the fight, but it looks cool, intimidating, and impressive. Next, he swings at the Djinn's head with one sword. The Djinn ducks the blades. Drew then uses his other sword to strike at the Djinn's legs, but the Djinn lifts one leg causing Drew to miss, bringing the weapons to his left side. He swings them back to the right to cut the Djinn, but the Djinn blocks them. For a second time, the swords clash, lock, and pause for a moment, then the Djinn jabs and cuts with his sword. Drew dodges and moves, always one move ahead of the Djinn, making it seem like he's twice as fast. He strikes back, missing the Djinn again and again. Then he leaps and tumbles to avoid the Djinn's blade while trying to hit him with his own. Finally, after a few more moments, the Djinn stabs Drew right through the center of his chest. The entire hologram obstacle course flashes and disappears.

All six Shadows run to Drew after he falls and hits the ground.

"You okay?" asks Wiz.

"Yeah, I'm fine," Drew replies. "They're just too fast! I don't know how I'm going to beat them."

"You looked faster than him for a second or two," Playmakers says.

"You can be twice as fast," Sifu Sun interrupts. "If you focus more."

"What does he mean?" asks Sky.

"Yeah, what does he mean?" echoes Tea.

"Well, my father has been helping me understand the quantum mechanic's theory of entanglement, the law of conservation of mass, and the law of conservation of energy," answers Drew.

Everyone stares at him, frowning. Drew sees the looks on their faces and takes the hint that he needs to explain. "The theory of entanglement," Drew continues, "says that all things are connected. They are still connected even if they are a million light years apart."

"Okay, but how does that explain you being faster than a superpowered Djinn?" asks Extra.

"The law of conservation mass says," Drew continues, "that mass is never really destroyed but only converted from one form to another. For example, we breathe oxygen and exhale carbon dioxide, then trees breathe carbon dioxide, and through photosynthesis, they make more oxygen."

"I'm hoping that eventually all of this mumbo jumbo will answer the question," Tea states.

Drew ignores her and continues, saying, "Finally, the law of energy conservation says that energy can never be destroyed but only converted from one form to another. For example—"

Wiz finishes Drew's comment by saying, "Electrical energy is converted into sound energy in a loudspeaker. Of course! And in a microphone, sound energy is converted into electrical energy. In a generator, mechanical energy is converted into electrical energy."

"If you don't tell us right now how this helps you be faster than a Djinn, then I'm gonna punch you right in the nose," says Extra.

"Okay, okay," answers Drew. "Through a process called Pathos, I can feel and even see how all energy is connected, and through the law of conservation mass, I can see the energy moving the mass.

"In other words," Wiz says, "you can tell where the Djinn will strike long before he does"

"Once his energy moves," Drew continues, "I can tell where it will end. That makes me appear to be faster than him."

"It works the same with the obstacle course. I can feel the vortex before it opens. The energy starts long before you can see it."

"That must be how you were able to stay on the solid squares," says Wiz.

"Yes," answers Drew. "Once the energy starts, I can feel where it will end."

"You said this power is called 'Pathos'?" asks Tea.

"Yup!" says Drew.

"Then that's what we'll call you," Tea says. She then looks at Extra, and they both nod.

"You shall hereby and forever more be called PATHOS the brave!" they say in unison.

"Let it be said," states Tea.

"Let it be so," agrees Extra.

They both laugh at their silly ceremony.

"Thanks," says Drew. "But we've already been using that name."

The girls look a little offended.

"How dare he use a new name before we have our ceremony?" says Extra.

"You'll all learn this power," announces Sifu Sun. "Your training here has been very successful. You are now ready for the next level."

At that moment, a haptic hologram drone appears above them. "There are intruders in the house, sir." It speaks in a female voice with a Chinese accent.

Sifu Sun gives a very stern look to everyone. Then, he stares a little longer at Drew and says, "All of you stay here!" He looks at Ms. Davis and says, "Make sure they stay here!" He walks over to the elevator shaft, gets into the lift, and pulls on the rope to lift himself to the house.

"Are you sure this is the place?" asks Ted Adams. He looks the exact same as he did at the campaign rally a few weeks ago. The only difference is that he wears a tan trench coat and a Trilby-style hat. In addition, a standard N95 mask covers his face.

"This is the address Remy gave me," Jake Slade answers. Jake is always dressed sharply. He feels that he always needs to look good just in case he runs into attractive ladies. He wears his N95 mask but doesn't like it. He thinks it hides his smile, and that's his best feature. The ladies can never resist his smile.

"Do we leave this here or wait for someone to come home?" asks Ted as he holds a piece of CrimCrystal in the shape of the letter T.

"There has to be a secret entrance around here," Jake says as he looks around the house.

Ted begins to help Jake look for the secret entrance that will take them more than twenty-six hundred feet below ground.

"Why can't we just leave this here and go?" asks Ted.

"Because not only do we have to give this to Sifu Sun Chang, but we also need to update everyone here on Remy's condition and the MC1 virus."

Windows shatter, doors burst open, and walls crash as several Djinn break their way into the house. Jake freezes and throws his hands in the air.

"We give up! We give up!" he screams.

"The hell we do!" shouts Ted.

Ted pulls his trench coat behind his waist like a gunslinger from the old west and draws two guns from the holsters on his hips. The guns look like six shooter revolvers, but when Ted pulls the trigger, red laser bolts come out of the barrel. The first bolt hits a Djinn in the head, knocking him upward and backward. He flies into a wall and hits the floor. Smoke lingers from the hole in his head. Ted continues to fire as Jake jumps behind a nearby bookshelf.

"You have laser pistols?" Jake shouts. "Who are you, man?"

Before Ted can answer, several Djinn shoot back with their own laser guns. Ted does an aerial no-handed cartwheel to dodge the bolts. Amazingly, he does all of this while shooting. He lands without a sound and quickly springs over the bookshelf. He crouches next to Jake as laser bolts fly over their heads, exploding behind them.

"You would think you know a guy after working with him for ten years," Jake says as he takes a laser pistol from Ted and starts firing back.

The shooting stops for a moment, then, a Djinn with a red tie says, "Give us the 'Pace of the Dunamai,' and we will allow you to live.

"The what?" asks Jake.

"They want this," Ted says as he holds up the T-shaped CrimCrystal. "You can have it over our dead bodies."

"Your!" Jake corrects him. "*Your* dead body! Leave my living body out of this."

"There are twenty of us out here," the red tie Djinn states. "We are stronger, faster, and more powerful than you. Do you really want to die over a relic you know nothing about?"

"No, we don't," answers Jake. "Give 'em the pace of the whatchamacallit, and let's get out of here!"

"You'll get nothing from us!" Ted shouts, as she starts shooting again.

Twenty Djinn aim at the bookshelf and fire all at once. The laser bolts blow up the bookshelf, throwing Ted several feet to the left and Jake several feet to the right. The room fills with debris, dust, and smoke. The

Djinn run to each side, looking for the men. They don't find either of them. It's as if they've vanished into thin air.

"Let them go," says the Djinn with the red tie. "Find the 'Pace of the Dunamai.'"

"Here it is," announces another Djinn as he holds up the CrimCrystal.

"Give it to me," demands the red-tie Djinn. As he reaches for it, the Djinn holding the Pace turns to smoke with a snap. The Pace falls to the floor, making a clanging sound.

"It's Kai," the red-tie Djinn warns. "Take cover!"

But before he can finish speaking, another Djinn turns to smoke as a CrimCrystal dagger flies through him and sticks in the wall. The room fills with black smoke, and streaks of glowing blue light fill the house. One by one, the Djinn turn to smoke. The Djinn with the red tie realizes he's next, so he grabs the Pace and dives for a window. He crashes through it and makes his escape.

Sifu Sun enters the room. Seeing the black smoke mixed with the lingering green smoke, he immediately knows Kai has been here. "Kai!" he shouts. A rustling of debris comes from behind him. He turns to see Jake struggling to get up.

"What happened?" Jake asks.

"Kai saved you," answers Sifu Sun. "Where's Ted?"

"I'm right here," Ted answers from the back of the room.

"Where were you?" asks Jake.

"I got knocked out," he answers. "What happened?"

"He said Kai saved us."

"Kai was here?" asks Ted.

"Why are you here?" asks Sifu Sun.

"We came to bring you something we found," answers Ted.

"Yea, it looks like it's made from the same stuff as a Caster," Jake adds.

"But it was a letter T," Ted explains.

"Well, it's gone now," Sifu Sun says.

"Where did you get those guns?" asks Jake. Ted looks at him but doesn't answer.

"And why do you always disappear when Kai is around? I'm starting to wonder if *you're* Kai!"

"Funny," Ted says. "I was just starting to think the same thing about you. So where were you when Kai showed up?"

"Gentlemen," Sifu Sun interrupts. "If your business is done here, then you should leave. There's still a very dangerous virus out there. None of us are safe. We should all be isolated until there's a cure."
"You're right," Ted says. "That's the other reason we're here: To give you an update on the virus and **Remy**."

"People are dying so fast that we can't bury them fast enough," Jake states. "As a result, the streets are littered with bodies, and the city is starting to stink like rotting flesh."

"Remy is in the hospital and still unconscious," Ted explains. "**We** don't know if it's the virus or something else, but if it's the virus, he's the only one who's lived past twenty-four hours with it."

"Whoever released the virus may have the vaccine," Sifu Sun explains. "Kai has been trying to figure that out. Until he does, we must stay inside and wait."

| 8 |

Pirate Plots

Listened for, He cannot be heard.

Baltimore, Maryland, USA. Thursday, August 21st, 2049, CE. 2:00 a.m. local time.

Kai crouches on the roof of an apartment building overlooking a dark and dangerous street. *Baltimore, Maryland,* he thinks to himself. *I hate coming here. But every clue about this MC1 virus has led me here. I bet there's a Djinn secret base nearby.*

People are dying from the MC1 virus so fast that the streets are littered with decaying bodies and the smell is unbearable. *All is quiet here,* Kai thinks to himself. *Too quiet!*

The shriek of a small girl breaks the eerie silence. "Spoke too soon," Kai whispers.

He turns to see a man enter the empty street. He's tall, wearing a black overcoat and hat that makes him look like the Djinn. He's dragging a little girl who screams while trying to escape him. Kai quickly does a front flip from the edge of the building. As he tumbles down, he spins like a circular saw and spews out small CrimCrystal-spiked balls. The spiked balls litter the man's chest as Kai lands directly in front of him without a sound.

"Wait!" the man says as he reaches into his coat pocket. "You don't underst—" the man's words are cut off as Kai stabs him in his shoulder with a CrimCrystal dagger. He falls forward to the ground, bleeding and yelling in pain. Kai is surprised; he expected the man to turn into a puff of green smoke.

"I thought you were a **Djinn**," Kai says in his metallic voice.

"A what?" The man's words are only grunts of pain as he lies on the ground holding his shoulder. He points at the girl and Kai turns to see her eyes glow green. She smiles with an evil grin and runs around the corner. Kai pursues her, turning the corner just in time to see the girl climbing up the wall of a nearby building as if she's an animal. She reaches the top and disappears onto the roof. Kai runs at full speed towards the building and leaps into the air. His arms spread wide like an eagle, his legs extend like a diver. Then, in mid-air, he pulls his knees to his chest, wraps his arms around them, and spins forward. After one complete front flip, he breaks open from his tucked position and flings *Toranado* towards an open window. Kai lands on the wall of the building and pushes himself back into the air with his feet, using *Toranado* to spring up to the top floor just short of the roof.

Kai perches on the ledge of a windowsill. It's old and weak from years of decay. When he lands on it, he realizes it won't hold him for long. He immediately begins to climb to the roof and look for the little girl. But suddenly, he hears a familiar voice coming through the window. It's the unmistakable deep, southern-Texas accent of Notorious, the Washington DC Pirates' gang leader.

Notorious stands before a room of the most evil-looking crowd Kai's seen in a long time. Notorious' appearance fits his name. He holds an unlit cigarette in his mouth and wears a black biker vest, a black t-shirt, and blue jeans with boots. On the back of his vest is a confederate flag.

Kip Eastland, Ren Kenji, and Axle Jones are standing behind Notorious in the front of the room as if they're his security guards. Among the thirty Pirate gang bangers in the room are Pirate leaders Sinister, Merciless, and Gore. They're infamous for their shocking cruelty. They sit in the far back, so the light doesn't shine directly on them. Notorious can only see a silhouette of each of them.

"If I tell ya I got a way to get rid of these Djinn and take over, then I mean it!" Notorious says.

"You think we're fools?" asks Sinister in his tenor Bronx accent.

"Let us hear what he has to say," states Gore. His voice is deep, and he speaks perfect English, pronouncing every word correctly.

"Now that the Djinn have released the virus, it's only gonna take a few months, then they're gonna rule the world. When that happens, all the governments and armies and stuff will be gone," Notorious explains.

"We know," Merciless states. "How does any of this help us overthrow the Djinn?"

"Well, since all of the world's governments will be gone, all we need to do is get rid of the Djinn, then we'll run thangs around here," Notorious explains.

"My patience is running out, boy!" Gore threatens.

"I had heard you were crazy, but now I know for sure," laughs Sinister. "The Djinn are superpowered. We would be fools to attack them! Plus, they're our allies. They gave the vaccine to us and all our gang members. So, give me one reason to betray them."

"What if we had a weapon that could identify and destroy Djinn? A weapon that's so powerful the Djinn have no defense against it," asks Notorious.

"There is no such weapon!" Merciless says.

"Not only is there such a weapon, but me and my boys are halfway there to finding it," Notorious explains.

"We are listening," says Gore as he leans back.

"Well, see, there are these books, two of 'em. One of 'em got written by these Djinn. The other got written by people like you and' me. Them two books together can tell us the location of this secret weapon. So, all we gotta do is get the books," Notorious finishes.

"And where are the books now?" asks Sinister.

"The Djinn have 'em," Notorious announces. Everyone in the room starts to mumble and complain.

"Now y'all calm down. Me and mah boys got a plan. We know exactly where one book is and how to get it. My boy Axle done told me Dr. Powers has an office underneath the Museum of Natural History. He said he saw the book on his desk."

"You are not just crazy. You are stupid," says Gore.

There's a moment of silence in the room, and then Sinister laughs hysterically. Hearing his laugh lets you know why people call him sinister. "I like it!" he exclaims. "You and your…boys—get the books," he says as he gets up to leave, "then call us."

"But that's why I called y'all here!" Notorious explains. "We need y'all's help to get the books." Then, after another pause, everyone in the room starts laughing.

At that moment, the windowsill that Kai is standing on breaks, and he falls, grabbing *Toranado* and crashing into the window, shattering glass everywhere.

"It's Kai!" Axle shouts.

Kai swings back to the outside of the window, climbs up *Toranado,* and disappears out of sight.

"Spread out and find him!" Notorious says.

"That ten million dollars is mine!" announces Sinister.

"Not if I find him first," says Merciless.

"I will litter the streets with his bones and fill the gutters with his blood," threatens Gore.

"Keep your AI speakers turned on and use the new toys the vaccine has given us," commands Ren.

"There he is!" Kip Eastland shouts as he looks up through the window.

"He's gonna have to come down through us!" Notorious explains. "The Pirate King is gonna be happier than a wet dog behind a warm stove when we catch Kai."

As Notorious gives orders, the crowd of Pirates begins to spread throughout the building. "Y'all move up floor by floor so he can't escape! If anyone sees him, then shout out!"

Meanwhile, on the roof, as he looks around the area, Kai thinks to himself, *a weapon that can destroy Djinn. I must get back and tell Sharon and Remy. We have go find those books*. He considers how he'll get out of the building without being caught. *It's too high to jump down the side. I'll have go down through the building, but I can't fight my way down. I don't know who's a Djinn and who's human, so I might accidentally kill a human.*

Kai remembers his father telling him, *"We never kill humans. We only stop Djinn. They're not supposed to be here now. This isn't their time. Their time has passed."*

I'll have to get to the bottom without being seen. He heads over to the electrical closet in the corner of the roof and breaks the doorknob with super strength. Next, he cuts the power to the whole building. *Let's see how well they can see in the dark,* he thinks to himself.

Below, the Pirates continue to spread out floor by floor, looking for Kai. The building is undergoing major construction. The floors are entirely open so that no walls separate the rooms. There are columns that go from the ceiling to the floor on each level. Tools, work benches, and piles of rubble and materials are everywhere. The Pirates move slowly, looking over and under objects, around columns, upwards to the ceilings, and in closets. Suddenly the lights go out, and it's pitch black.

"Switch to night vision," commands Notorious.

Kip, Ren, and Axle speak the words "Night vision." They can instantly see in the dark. They don't wear helmets, glasses, or any gear. They can just see out of their own eyes in the dark. Every Pirate does the same and can now see in the dark too.

Kai drops into the fourth floor from a hole in the ceiling, thinking he'll be undetected because it's dark and he's wearing all black.

"There he is!" shouts Ren. "Over in the corner!" All Pirates turn and fire their laser guns. Kai drops a smoke bomb and is gone in an instant.

Laser guns, he thinks. *Those can probably kill me. I must be very careful now.* Good thing his training with Sifu Sun has paid off. That was unexpected, and it nearly cost him his life.

The smoke hides Kai, and he's quiet as a cat. No one can hear him even though he's only inches away from the people he passes. He pauses when he finds the opening that he needs to drop to the third floor. *Oh no, not this time*, he thinks to himself. He throws ten smoke bombs onto the third floor. The entire floor fills with black smoke. Kai drops down, lands without a sound, and begins to walk undetected between Djinn. Once again, they can't see or hear him. He moves like a ninja, taking careful, slow, quiet steps. Everyone is tense, focused, and quiet. No one knows how dangerous Kai is. And Kai doesn't know if these weapons will kill him or not. The slightest noise could cause someone to start shooting.

Kai quietly steps through the smoke only to turn around to find himself face-to-face with Notorious. Although Notorious can't see him, he seems to be able to feel Kai's presence. Kai holds his breath as Notorious reaches out to touch him. He barely ducks in time, and Notorious misses.

"Glass!" Notorious shouts into his AI link. "Cover the floor in broken glass. We'll be able to hear him when he steps on it." The Pirates on every floor begin to shoot out the windows and break whatever glass they can find.

When the second floor fills with black smoke, an unidentified Pirate voice says, "He's on the second floor."

"Everyone, head to the first floor. Break Glass!" Notorious shouts.

A few moments later, Notorious stands on the sidewalk in front of the building. Behind him are the silhouettes of Gore, Sinister, and Merciless.

"He's gone," says Merciless.

"I don't understand how! The first floor was never filled with smoke. He must be in that building somewhere," says Notorious.

"He must be an ancient warrior," explains Sinister. "It's said of the ancient warriors, 'Looked for, they cannot be seen….'"

"'Listened for they cannot be heard….'" Gore continues Sinister's sentence.

"'Reached for, they cannot be touched,'" Merciless completes the idiom.

| 9 |

The YellowJackets

Metropolitan Police Headquarters—the Henry J. Daly Building in Washington DC, USA. Monday, August 24th, 2049, CE. 7:01 p.m. local time.

Officer Bill, Chief Harris, Mani Dradow, and Pastor Seth sit playing cards just down the hall from jailed prisoners. Each wears an N95 mask and latex gloves.

"Thank you for being here, guys," the chief says.

"I've nothing better to do," answers Officer Bill in his Scottish accent.

"I figured you would need a little help down here," says Pastor Seth in his usual grumpy tone. "I don't think you have many policemen who want to be out while this virus is going on."

"Yes, yes," Mani says. "Quite true indeed. I need to be here until we can move Mike Nicholson. That guy gives me the willies. Bad blood he is. Very bad blood."

"And right now, would be the perfect time for his criminal friends to try and break him out," explains Pastor Seth.

"A lot of help you'll be in a wheelchair," Chief Harrison says.

"Maybe I should just go home then," Pastor Seth shoots back.

"Oh, I'm sorry, I didn't mean that," says the chief. "I'm just a little on edge with this virus thing."

"You aren't worried about Nicholson escaping?" asks Mani.

"I assure you, we are very safe here," the chief answers.

Suddenly there's a loud boom. The entire building shakes so hard that Mani and the chief fall.

"Tell us again how safe we are," smirks Pastor Seth.

"What was that?" asks the chief.

They hear and feel more banging as something hits the wall. This time they hear crackling sounds as the outer wall begins to crumble.

"Get me out of here!" Pastor Seth says with more anger than usual.

Mani is a small man, and Pastor Seth is a large man, so Mani struggles as he pushes him outside. They see the cause of the noise once they get outside. In the dusk of the day, a huge man is standing on the corner of the building punching the wall. This man is seven feet six inches tall. He has long, bushy black hair, which falls just below his shoulders and covers most of his face. He wears no shirt. There are metal cuffs on his wrists, and like a Genie, he has long harem pants with black leather boots.

"That's the one from the news," says Pastor Seth. "The one everyone has been looking for. They called him Gideon." Pastor Seth notices that the green amulet hanging from Gideon's neck is glowing brighter than ever as the day turns to night.

Outside of the building are several Djinn dressed exactly like the hologram. They've surrounded the area, armed with guns and short swords. When they see Pastor Seth, they stare at him in awkward silence.

"We need to get out of here!" Mani says as he tries to turn the wheelchair. He hurries down the street, hoping the Djinn don't chase them. As they leave, they hear the familiar bang again. Gideon has punched through the outer wall and is now pounding the steel interior.

Chief Harrison and Officer Bill exit the police station. Several Djinn point guns at them, so they put their hands up and fall to their knees. A few Djinn take them behind parked cars as Gideon lands his final punch. He breaks through the metal wall, rips the hole wider, and climbs through it. A moment later, Gideon emerges from the same hole carrying Mike by the back of his collar. He heads west down Indiana street, and all the Djinn follow—some on foot and others in black SUVs.

In the commotion, Officer Bill has disappeared, and Chief Harrison is left alone, still hiding behind a parked car. Harrison stands up and dusts the dirt from the street off his clothes. *Where did Bill go? How does he always disappear like that?* After a moment or two, he returns to the building, calls more police officers to help, and notifies the mayor of a jail breakout.

"I have them on scanners. It looks like they're leaving," HallowPoint announces over the commlink in her car.

Five very unusual cars called '*Ultra*' head down Third Street on their way to the police station. Each *Ultra* is painted yellow with black trim. What makes the *Ultra's* unusual is that they don't have regular wheels. Instead of tires, they have giant balls or spheres for wheels. The balls don't touch the frame of the car. Instead, they're suspended in mid-air on the outside of the car. Each wheel is six feet high from its bottom to its top, so they lift the oval frame of the car three feet off the ground. The cars' frames are three feet wide and five feet long. In the center of the *Ultra* is a glass ball where the driver sits. The driver's seat is suspended in mid-air inside the glass ball. The ball is three feet from its center to its edge. Around the edges of the frame are several vents that blow air to make the car go super-fast.

"EL Caballero, you and Tombstone head down Indiana Street," Breeze commands. "Me and HallowPoint will go down C Street to cut them off," she continues. Her country accent is distinct and alluring.

"What about me?" asks The Challenge. He has a deep tenor voice and an upscale English accent.

"Improvise," answers Breeze. "And everyone, turn on your lights. It's almost dark."

They follow orders, and soon the five *Ultra's* wheels and rear lights glow blue while white headlight beams appear in the front of the cars. Each car hits the accelerator and speeds towards the police station. At the first corner, all five turn left in a one-by-two-by-two formation. At the second corner EL Caballero (in *Ultra* 4) and Tombstone (in *Ultra* 5) make a sharp right to head to the other side of the police building. Breeze (in *Ultra* 1), HallowPoint, (in *Ultra* 2), and The Challenge (in *Ultra* 3) continue straight down C street. Breeze is leading the way. The *Ultras* roll over parked cars, crushing them as they speed down the road.

"There they are," TombStone announces in a thick Mexican accent. His voice is lifeless and cold, almost as if he's dead.

"Tiempo de fiesta!" EL Caballero grumbles through gritted teeth. His accent is like his half-brother's but sounds more Spanish than Mexican.

They gain quickly on at least one hundred Djinn following Gideon down Indiana Street. As they get closer to the Djinn, Breeze notices they seem to be heading toward the Washington Monument.

"Use the tandem CrimCrystal cables," commands Breeze.

"YellowJackets!" Gideon exclaims in irritation as he sees two *Ultra* cars chasing them. He looks at the Djinn while pointing at the YellowJackets and commands, "GET 'EM!"

EL Caballero releases a CrimCrystal cable from a side vent on his car. The glowing cable shoots out and connects with a vent on Tombstone's car. They both zoom down the road, crushing more parked cars.

Several Djinn stop running to turn and face the oncoming *Ultras*. They draw guns and fire, but the *Ultras* keep coming with the CrimCrystal rope fully extended between them. The rope cuts through several of the Djinn as the giant sphere wheels of the *Ultras* run over others. The Djinn turn to smoke as their bodies are split at the waist by the cable, but the Djinn that are run over are unharmed. They get up and continue to shoot at the YellowJacket cars. There's so much smoke that they can barely be seen when the streetlights come on.

After the two cars pass through the Djinn, they release the rope and split up. Tombstone keeps straight and heads down D Street, while EL Caballero turns left down Sixth Street, heading south. Breeze and HallowPoint drive up Sixth Street north. They come face-to-face with each other at full speed.

HallowPoint has super speed, so she swerves and misses EL Caballero. However, Breeze is unable to avoid hitting him. To avoid the crash, EL Caballero presses a button on his controls, causing the front of his car to bounce upward. He lands on HallowPoint's car and drives over it. The impact causes his *Ultra* to do a front flip. Because EL Caballero's driver's seat is suspended in mid-air, he remains upright while the car flips around him. The giant sphere wheels allow the car to land and keep going.

"Watch where you're going!" shouts Breeze.

"This was not *my* game plan," El Caballero reminds her.

The crash delays Breeze and HallowPoint long enough for Gideon, still dragging Mike, to pass the place where Breeze wanted to cut them off. Breeze and HallowPoint turn left onto Indiana Street and continue the chase. When they turn northwest onto Pennsylvania Ave., they can see that Gideon is now several hundred yards in front of them.

"Release the Nephilim!" Gideon commands.

Several miles from where the YellowJackets chase the Djinn is a large metal circle in the ground. The circle begins to split in the middle and slide apart. Under it is a secret place the government used to hide missiles. Four Giants climb out of it and head toward Gideon.

Breeze and HallowPoint are gaining on Gideon. To slow them down, three Djinn stop their cars and block the road. They get out of their cars, stand behind them, and shoot at the speeding *Ultras*. The *Ultras* slam into the cars flipping them forward at the same time. The cars explode when on impact, lighting up the night sky. The *Ultras* flip front, sideways, and diagonal before landing on their giant wheels. The drivers remain upright while the cars spin around them.

"I want Gideon!" Breeze demands after her car lands.

"Too late!" The Challenge says. He's heading southeast on Pennsylvania Ave., directly for Gideon. "You snooze, you lose."

"How did you get over there?" asks Breeze.

"You said improvise," he answers.

"Okay, so let's improvise," Breeze says to HallowPoint.

Breeze shoots out a CrimCrystal cable from the side of her car and connects with HallowPoint. The two cars zoom toward the Djinn at the same time.

"Smoke 'em if you got 'em," HallowPoint says as they turn the Djinn following Gideon into smoke.

At about the same time, The Challenge shoots CrimCrystal bullets at Gideon. Gideon, while holding Mike, does a standing, no-hand cartwheel over the bullets and lands just in front of the *Ultra* 3 as it speeds toward him. The Challenge turns his steering wheel sharply to avoid hitting the large Djinn, but Gideon is ready and kicks the side of the car with all his might. The car tumbles sideways down Pennsylvania Ave.

Again, The Challenge stays upright in his suspended seat. His car finally comes to a stop several hundred feet away.

"You're gonna pay for that!" The Challenge says.

"I may. But not today," Gideon smiles.

Behind Gideon, *Ultra* 1 and *Ultra* 2 are mowing down Djinn with their CrimCrystal rope, heading straight for him. However, in front of him and behind The Challenge, four Giants, each twenty feet tall, are running toward Gideon. They wear gold harem pants with a sash around the waist. One sash is blue, another black, another green, and one yellow. Their shirts, fit like pirates' shirts, are white and hang open in the front, showing their muscular chests. Over their heads is a black hood connected to a long cloak that falls to the back of their knees as they run down Pennsylvania Ave., covering ten yards per step.

"Crush the YellowJackets!" Gideon commands as the four Giants arrive on the scene.

| 10 |

The Battle of the Nephilim

Near the National Children Museum, Washington DC, USA. Monday, August 24th, 2049, CE. 8:15 p.m. local time.

"Are you freakin' kidding me right now?" Breeze says.

"Looks like the Amulet of Zahra finds more than just Djinn," HallowPoint states.

"Can we take 'em?" asks Breeze.

"Challenge accepted," he says as he turns his car around.

Gideon takes off running towards the National Monument, still carrying Mike. It's hard to see him now that it's dark, but the streetlights help.

"Where do you think you're going, mi amigo," EL Caballero says. He and TombStone show up just in time.

"Gideon is mine," says Breeze. "You two help take care of these Nephilim."

Breeze disconnects her rope from HallowPoint's car and speeds toward Gideon. Out of nowhere, a giant hand slams down onto Breeze's car to stop completely. The Giant kicks the *Ultra* 1 into the air and it crashes into a building. Breeze tries to drive the car out of the rubble but can't. She is stuck.

"Somebody stop Gideon!" Breeze shouts. "He is getting away!"

Gideon runs faster as he heads towards the White House visitor center and Pershing Park. Suddenly a rope with weights on each end wraps around his ankles, causing him to stumble and fall over. He accidentally drops Mike as he hits the ground.

Gideon hears someone say, "Going someplace?" He rolls over on the ground to see the hooded figure of Pathos.

"I will rip you apart for this," Gideon threatens.

"Bring it!" Pathos replies.

Gideon breaks the ropes around his ankles and charges toward Pathos, who runs back to Thirteenth Street. He turns down the dimly lit walkway heading to the National Children's Museum. He has a head start, but Gideon gains on him quickly. He stops once he's in the courtyard, just past the museum entrance.

Fueled by rage, and focused on ripping Pathos apart, Gideon turns down the walkway, running as fast as he can. Suddenly he feels blinding pain from being kicked in the head. The blow knocks him sideways and sends him crashing through a window of the museum. With anger and fury, Gideon roars as he gets up. He's bleeding from glass cuts but glowing green in the eyes.

"I will grind your bones to make my bread," he growls. He turns to see who kicked him. To his surprise it's THE MIGHTY KAI! "YOU!" he exclaims.

"Boy, he sure is ugly when he's mad," Pathos says.

"This is no laughing matter," Kai warns. "He's dangerous, so stay focused."

At that moment, Gideon roars again and charges at Kai, who quickly dodges to the right. Gideon falls over the large silver statue of a rose in the courtyard, then over the Woodrow Wilson wall, and right down to the pavement of the patio twelve feet below. His eyes stop glowing, because all his superpower energy gone.

"I think you upset him," says Kai.

"Me?" asks Pathos. "What did I do?"

Kai and Pathos walk to the wall and peek over to see if they can see Gideon. Street lamps light up the patio below, but it's still dim and hard to see. As they lean over, Gideon jumps twelve feet and punches Kai causing him to fly backward and hit the ground hard. Gideon lands on the wall with eyes glowing green, fists clenched, and his muscles tightened.

"Finally, I will finish the King's command and end you!" Gideon says as he looks at Kai, who is slowly getting up.

Gideon stands seven feet six inches, while Pathos is five feet tall. Gideon stands on the wall, making him even taller as Pathos still stands on the ground. When Pathos does a roundhouse kick, it only lands on Gideon's shin.

"Ouch!" Pathos exclaims as he grabs his foot.

"I will squash you like a bug," Gideon threatens.

He jumps off the wall, intending to crush Pathos. However, he dodges just in the nick of time, and Gideon cracks the cement when he lands.

Three-foot-tall cement safety pillars are in front of the Woodrow Wilson wall. Pathos leaps onto one of them and kicks Gideon in the face. He barely feels the blow and swings back at Pathos but misses. Pathos leaps from pillar to pillar, barely dodging Gideon's attacks.

"Now!" says Pathos as Gideon misses again.

Kai takes the queue from Pathos and does a flying kick to Gideon's head for a second time, knocking him back over the wall and down to the pavement again. Next, Kai pulls out his CrimCrystal daggers and leaps over the wall in a front-flip dive, intending to stab Gideon, but he rolls out of the way, and Kai stabs the pavement instead.

Pathos knows he can never make that jump, so he heads for the stairs. As he makes his way down the stairs, Gideon stands up with his eyes glowing green again.

"Uh oh," says Kai as a punch knocks him through the windows of a nearby shop. Electricity buzzes, and several lights go out, making the patio darker.

Gideon turns and corners Pathos on the stairs. He swings, but Pathos does a front tuck over his arm and lands behind him. He pulls his swords from their sheaths and stabs Gideon with both in his back. Gideon turns and laughs as the pain causes his glow to extend down his neck, chest, and arms. Pathos is so stunned that he loses focus long enough for Gideon to reach out and pick him up.

"Put him down," Kai says as he emerges from the broken window, his eyes glowing blue. His voice is no longer lighted-hearted or joking. It's okay if the Djinn hurt him, but not if they hurt his friends.

"As you wish," Gideon says. He tosses Pathos like a rag doll through the glass-covered roof, which knocks out more lighting. Pathos hits a wall with a thump and falls lifelessly to the ground.

Anger rushes through Kai. The fear that Gideon is too powerful is gone. He pulls several daggers from his belt and throws them at the remaining lights. One by one, the lights shatter, leaving them in darkness. The only things they can see in the dark are their glowing eyes.

Kai unsheathes his newly repaired sword and attacks. In mid-swing, Gideon grabs the sword by the blade while Kai still holds the handle. He pauses a moment as he examines the blade closely. Kai tries to pull it away from him but fails.

"This is not the Crimson sword," he says. "Without it, you are no match for me!" He then squeezes his hand and shatters the blade. The super-powered move uses all his energy, and the glow in his eyes is gone.

Kai drops a smoke bomb as he feels his power growing from his wrath. His fists glow to match his eyes, and he punches Gideon with all his might. The punch flashes blue in the darkness, and for a split second, Gideon's face is x-rayed, and Kai sees his jawbone fracture. Kai strikes again and again with all of his fury and might. Each hit makes a blue flash so that the patio area looks like blue lightning is striking. The blows land and knock Gideon off balance. Kai sees a trickle of blood spurt from his lips as he lands a right cross to his ribs. The hit x-rays his ribs, giving a glimpse of them shattering. Gideon screams in pain and falls. **Q**uickly, Kai swings again and again before Gideon can recover. Finally, Kai's super energy is gone, and he no longer glows.

"I don't need a sword to defeat you," Kai says.

Gideon rises to his feet with blood trickling from his nose and mouth. His eye is swollen red and black, and there's a sharp pain in his side with every breath. "You need more than a sword to defeat me," smiles Gideon. "You need *the* sword of power, and you don't have it."

Kai tries to punch him, but this time Gideon catches his fist in midair. Gideon smiles an evil grin as he cocks his arm back so far that his fist is behind his head. He hits Kai with all his might. Green flashes in the darkness. Kai feels pain from the wounds that haven't fully healed from his fight with Ominous only a few weeks ago. Finally, Gideon hits him in his gut, causing him to cough up blood.

Kai falls to his knees. He has no defense left; he used up his superpower too quickly. His body is exhausted from fighting weeks before and today. His will is gone, and he realizes he's at Gideon's mercy. Gideon sees the defeat in his eyes, so he picks him up and throws him hard into a nearby wall. Kai hits the wall with a thump and slowly slides down to the ground. Gideon picks up the daggers Kai left on the ground.

"Is this what you planned to use to stop me?" he asks as he holds up the daggers. He walks over to Kai and lifts him from the ground. Kai's arms and legs dangle lifelessly. He holds a dagger to Kai's throat and says, "I could smoke you here and now, but I won't. First, I need to make an example out of you."

Meanwhile, the Giants square off with the YellowJackets on Fifteenth Street in front of Pershing Park. CrimCrystal bullets bounce off the Giants as the YellowJackets shoot at them.

"Why aren't they turning into giant green smoke?" asks EL Caballero as the yellow Giant picks up the *Ultra* 4 and repeatedly slams it into the side of the Commerce Research Library.

"Their skin is too thick," answers Tombstone as he and his car soar through the air from the green Giant's kick. He flies several hundred feet and lands on the White House's south lawn. The Giant runs to find him, crashing through the nearby statue of General Sherman.

"We need a way to penetrate their skin," says Breeze. Unfortunately, she's still stuck in the side of the building. However, she's maneuvering her *Ultra* back and forth, trying to break free.

"Challenge accepted," says The Challenge as he zooms under the black Giant. The Giant reaches for him but barely misses, so he tries to stomp on the car. Fortunately, the *Ultra* 3 is too fast, and the Giant misses with each stomp.

At that moment, bullets rain from the sky, hitting the yellow Giant, who is still repeatedly banging EL Caballero's *Ultra* 4 into the side of the building. The US military has arrived with F-16 fighter jets. The intersection fills with soldiers and six army tanks. The soldiers throw grenades and shoot automatic rifles at the Giants.

"Who invited them?" asks The Challenge.

"There are always party crashers," says Breeze.

"Do you want us to take the military out?" asks HallowPoint as she fires at the blue Giant.

"No, we'll deal with the humans after we defeat the Djinn," Breeze explains as she tries to free her *Ultra* 1.

The yellow Giant drops the *Ultra* 4 and jumps into the air, swatting at an F-16. He hits it, and the fighter jet comes crashing down and explodes. Immediately two tanks fire at the Giant. The rockets hit him, but they only make him growl in pain and fall over onto the building. The side of the building crumbles under the weight of the Giant. He knocks down the rest of the building as he stumbles to his feet. More rockets hit him, making him roar in pain again.

"They can jump!" a fighter pilot says over the radio. "Raise your altitude."

The F-16s hovering over the area fly higher in the air. The black Giant jumps and swipes at one of them, but the plane is too high now. Now both tanks and F-16's fire at him, knocking him down.

The blue Giant becomes enraged and rips a fully-grown tree out of the ground. Its roots are hanging from the bottom, along with clumps of dirt. Moreover, dust falls as he lifts it. He throws it at the planes, and it hits an F-16, knocking it out of the sky. The yellow Giant does the same thing, knocking down another F-16.

"Clear the square," a pilot says. "We're switching to missiles."

The tanks back away, and the soldiers run for cover.

"A little help over here, please," Tombstone says as the green Giant clears the trees and enters the White House's south lawn.

"I'm on my way," HallowPoint answers. She has the blue Giant right on her tail.

Breeze reroutes power to the air vents in her car and slams on the gas. The extra power allows her to pop out of the hole in the building. The car finally tumbles down and lands on the pavement.

"Yes, back in action!" she says. "I'm on my way to you too."

The F-16s fire missiles, hitting the blue and black Giants. Both fall to the ground. Soldiers and tanks fire so rapidly that you can't see the Giants under the fire and smoke.

"I have a plan," says El Caballero.

"I was thinking the same thing," agrees Tombstone.

Together the half-brothers say, "Lure them to the open field."

The yellow Giant throws a tree at the F-16s but notices that the tanks have his brothers trapped under fire. He runs to a tank and stomps on it. The tank explodes, killing the soldiers in it. He picks up a second tank and crushes it with his bare hands. Soldiers on the ground run for cover as their commanding officer yells for them to retreat, then the F-16s turn their firepower on the yellow Giant. This frees his two brothers so they can attack the YellowJackets again.

"Everyone, come to the White House's south law," says Tombstone. "And make sure the Giants follow you."

|11|

Finish Him

Near the White House south lawn, Washington DC, USA. Monday, August 24th, 2049, CE. 9:05 p.m. local time.

Four *Ultras* race to the White House's south lawn to meet Tombstone. Breeze leads the way. Their glowing cars mow down trees and parked cars as they go. Behind them, four Giants pursue. Behind the Giants, army tanks and soldiers chase and shoot. In the air, F-16s hover and fire at the Giants when they can get a clear shot. Military helicopters have shown up and are flooding the south lawn with light from the air. Finally, news helicopters have appeared and are broadcasting the fight to every TV and smart device in the world.

Sharon watches, sitting alone at home. She simply cannot believe what she's seeing. Real life Giants. *What is the world coming to?*

Two nurses and one doctor stand gazing at the monitor watching the Giants attack the White House on TV. They watch the TV so intensely that they don't notice the bed behind them is empty. They're in Remy's room. He's gone.

Sifu Sun has the Shadows all lined up going through exercises for their training. Because there is no reception underground, they're totally unaware of what's going on at the White House. They keep training as if it's just another day.

Pathos is passed out right where Gideon threw him into the wall.

"We're here live," the newscaster says from the helicopter. "Where it appears that several Giants are attacking the White House."

The *Ultras* break through trees and into the clearing.

"Pair up," Tombstone says. "We'll use the cables on them."

"Will that work?" asks HallowPoint as she moves her *Ultra* 2 beside Breeze, in *Ultra* 1, so that they can link CrimCrystal cables.

"It will have to," El Caballero answers. "It's the only thing we have that might penetrate their skin."

"Well, you're gonna have to slow 'em down," The Challenge says as he clears the broken trees and enters the south lawn.

The black Giant runs through the trees into the clearing. The other Giants are right behind him. As soon as they're in the clearing, the F-16s start shooting at them. The Giants roar, rip fully grown trees out of the ground and start throwing them at the planes. They barely miss the news helicopter. Some of the planes go crashing down. The Giants run through the field, chasing the planes. They seem to have forgotten about the YellowJackets for the moment.

The black Giant reaches the White House and climbs to the roof so he can get high enough to reach the planes. Tanks and F-16s start to fire at him as he jumps to knock the planes out of the sky. The White House takes on damage and the roof is filled with holes from the explosions.

The army tanks and soldiers reach the south lawn clearing. They immediately set up flood lights so they can see the Giants.

"I can slow them down," says Tombstone. His voice has turned ice cold and dead. His eyes go white and there's a crackle of thunder in the clear night sky. Dozens of corpses begin to claw their way out of the ground. They run to the Giants and start climbing up their bodies and biting them.

"Slaves," EL Caballero says. "This ground is littered with them."

The black Giant falls through the roof of the White House, but he gets back up and climbs out of the rubble to help his brothers fight off the zombie slaves.

Tombstone and EL Caballero pair up to use the cables against the Giants.

"Rest in peace," TombStone says as the two *Ultra's* hook up their CrimCrystal rope. They drive up behind the yellow Giant and cut right through the back of his leg with their rope. The Giant falls over, screaming in pain. His severed foot sits on the grass alone.

"I don't get it," says EL Caballero. Why no puff of smoke? He didn't turn into a puff of smoke. I want my smoke!"

"The Nephilim have different blood than the Djinn," explains The Challenge. "Maybe CrimCrystal doesn't work on them."

"Everyone, hit him while he's down!" commands Breeze. The other YellowJackets obey. They zoom around the reach of the three still-standing Giants and head for the fallen one. As they arrive, they hear the yellow Giant begin to scream. His body trembles, and then he explodes. Pink goo lands everywhere. The White House, the grass, the trees, the Giants, and even the YellowJackets are covered in it.

"Okay, so we know it works. Let's turn 'em into goo," commands Breeze.

Breeze and HallowPoint sever the foot of the green Giant while Tombstone and EL Caballero do the same with the blue and black Giants. A few moments later, pink goo explodes everywhere. The Giants are defeated, and the zombie slaves have returned to their graves under the White House lawn. There are cheers coming from the soldiers and newscasters in the helicopter. People watching all over the world cheer. The YellowJackets cheer.

"Ahora que es una fiesta," says EL Caballero.

"Yes!" Shouts HallowPoint.

"I think Gideon got away," observes Breeze.

"With Mike, and the book of the Djinn," The Challenge says.

At that moment, Gideon comes onto the lawn from the broken trees. He carries Kai over his shoulder. Kai seems to have passed out. Blood trickles from his facemask and down his arms to the tip of his fingers.

Sharon falls to her knees in front of her TV. She covers her mouth with her hands and tears begin to fall from her eyes. "No," she whispers.

"Maybe there's still a chance," says Tombstone as the YellowJackets move their cars into attack position.

"Wait," says breeze. "Be careful. Kai is the only one who can defeat the Djinn. We need him."

"Is this your hope?" asks Gideon as he holds up Kai's lifeless body.

The news helicopter is still broadcasting. The army has held its position and they watch to see what Gideon will do with the notorious Mighty Kai.

"Today, that hope ends!" he says as he pulls out one of Kai's CrimCrystal daggers. Gideon savors the moment. He loves all the attention he's getting. Every eye around the world is now on him. Plus, he will finally fulfill the command of King Nefarious, and kill Kai. This is a moment to be remembered.

Gideon's eyes glow lime green as he holds Kai high over his head. The daggers glow blue. With all his strength, he rams the dagger into Kai's lifeless body. Kai instantly turns to blue smoke that drifts away into the night sky.

Sharon feels her body go limp. Gideon may as well have stabbed her. She sits on her knees, sobbing.

"No!" Breeze shouts.

"You monster!" cries HallowPoint.

"Well, that's unfortunate," states The Challenge.

"Do you want us to take him down?" asks EL Caballero.

"No," answers Breeze. The army will do that for us. Let's get out of here."

The five YellowJackets zoom out of sight in their *Ultra* cars. Gideon is left alone with guns, tanks, and F-16s pointing at him. He puts his hands on his head, drops to his knees, and surrenders.

| 12 |

The Vaccine

The National Museum of Natural History, Washington DC. Tuesday, August 26th, 2049, CE. 9:00 a.m. local time.

Dr. Stephen Powers stands in his secret room, waiting for world leaders to log in to the video chat. Most of them are not here yet.

"Is this all that's coming?" he asks.

"Start your meeting, Powers," President King says. "We're the only world leaders still alive."

"Very well," Dr. Powers replies. "Are you ready to give control of your countries to the Harvest?"

"I met with congress," President King says. "Or, at least, what's left of them. We're dying so fast that soon, there won't be a government to hand over. So, we have agreed to do whatever it takes to save lives. Our country is yours once you provide a safe vaccine."

"We're all in agreement, Dr. Powers," announces Prime Minister Davies. "But the vaccine must be released now!"

"The vaccine will first go to you, your staff, and then to the people," Dr. Powers answers. "Also, don't tell anyone about the Harvest. The people need to live normally. Does everyone understand?"

"Yes! Anything you want, just give us the vaccine!" supreme leader Kim Kye-Chul demands.

"How long will it take for you to give us the vaccine?" asks President King.

"Our agents are bringing them to you now," Dr. Powers explains. "Make sure everyone takes one pill."

"A pill?" asks Chancellor Schmidt.

"Yes," answers Dr. Powers. "The vaccine is in a pill, not a shot."

"Why should we trust you? How do we know this pill will work? What if it kills us?" asks Kim Kye-Chul.

"What choice do we have?" argues President King.

"I have a person who will surely die within the hour," President Wei says. "I will give it to him first to see if it works."

"How long will it take to see results?" asks Prime Minister Davies.

"You will see results instantly," answers Dr. Powers. "Anyone who takes the vaccine will be healed within the hour, no matter how sick they are."

Dr. Powers watches the holograms as his agents enter the background to drop off pills. The agents are Djinn.

Almost twenty minutes go by before President Wei returns. "It works!" he says with excitement. "I've already taken mine."

Dr. Powers opens the control panel. On it are millions of names of people. Next to the names are red lights. Every so often, a red light turns green, meaning someone has taken the vaccine and is now online. Dr. Powers scrolls through the screen to find all the world leaders. Once all their lights are green, Dr. Powers announces, "Later today, tell the people that a vaccine will be delivered to their homes."

"You will deliver to five billion homes?" asks President Wei.

"We have drones that can make the deliveries," answers Dr. Powers.

Suddenly everyone hears laughter. Dr. Powers scrolls through the holograms looking for whoever's laughing. It's Chancellor Schmidt. Then more people start to laugh with him.

"Just what…is *so* amusing?" asks Dr. Powers.

"You fool!" answers Chancellor Schmidt. "Did you really think we would give you our countries after we have the vaccine? You've made this too easy!" he says, still laughing.

More world leaders join his laughter while nodding their heads. However, President King still has a serious look on her face. "Let us have some order, people," she says. "We've been meeting secretly over the last two weeks to decide what to do with you, Dr. Powers. I'll make this short and simple: you will be tried for treason, and the Harvest will be hunted down…."

Grunts of pain and coughing cut off her words. Chancellor Schmidt can't breathe.

"Did you think we were that dumb?" asks Dr. Powers. "To give you the vaccine without a foolproof backup plan?"

The coughing gets louder as Dr. Powers speaks.

"We know about your secret meetings," Dr. Powers continues, "and we are well prepared. There will be a new UWG, and you can't stop it." No one understands the UWG, so he explains, "The UNIVERSAL WORLD GOVERNMENT."

Chancellor Schmidt begins to cough up blood.

"The vaccine has a chip that we control," Dr. Powers explains. "When you swallowed that pill, you installed a chip in your blood. We can use that chip to stop your heartbeat, breathing, and everything else inside your body. So, if anyone disobeys us, this will be your punishment."

At that moment, Chancellor Schmidt falls over dead.

"Do I need to make another example or are we clear?" asks Dr. Powers. No one says a word. "Good!"

President King finally speaks up and asks, "So what happens now?"

"As I said before," Dr. Powers answers. "The people need to live normally, so give them the vaccine, and each of you will be heroes. Over the next few months, the countries will be changed into seven provinces based on the seven continents. We'll leave local governments in place, like police, sheriffs, prisons, and schools. However, new laws, technology, and a Universal World Government will exist. There will be one law for the whole world. And the Djinn shall rule."

Who Will Collect the Reward?

For More Information, visit us at
www.whoisthemightykai.com

Follow Us

TikTok
tiktok.com/@whoisthemightykai

Youtube
https://www.youtube.com/@whoisthemightykai

Facebook
@whoisthemightykai

Instagram
@the_mightykai

Twitter
@the_mightykai

Linked In
www.linkedin.com/in/themightykai

Website
Http://www.whoisthemightykai.com
Http://www.omnieyeentertainment.com

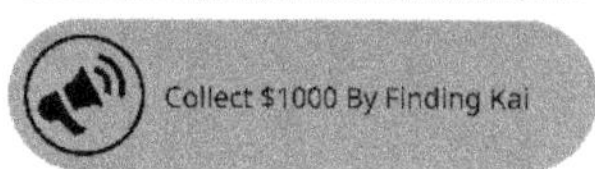

About the Author

Kennon D. Olison Sr. started his career as a minister of the gospel of Jesus Christ in Bakersfield CA. Being a writer is not something he set out to do, however, he recognized that very few of his colleagues in ministry were writing down their knowledge for future generations. That was when he decided to place his studies in a formal volume. His first work is entitled "Music in Worship; An Examination of the Contemporary Music in the church of Christ." That work is still used by various churches of Christ around the world as a classroom curriculum.

Kennon has always had a love for comics and fiction. A love he passed on to his sons, KJ and Evan. He has had a long ambition to create his own comic book universe, but time never permitted. In 2020 the pandemic hit and shut down the world. Suddenly, there was nothing but time, and it was then that he finally sat down and put his dreams on paper.

Go get 'em Kennon. Shoot for the moon! If you miss, you will be among the stars.

The Origin Story!

Order your copy today at
www.whoisthemightykai.com

Includes Clue #2

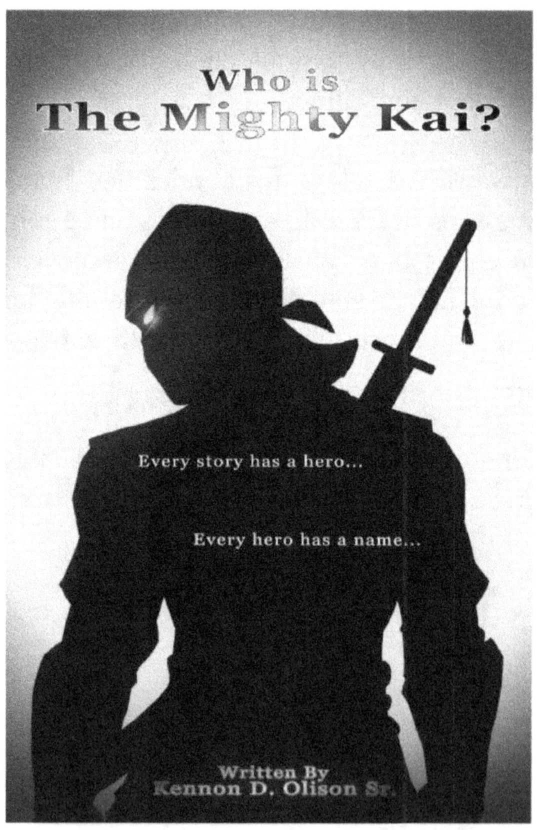

Available Now!

Order your copy today at
www.whoisthemightykai.com

Includes Clue #1

Coming Soon!

For More Information, visit us at
www.whoisthemightykai.com

Will contain Clue's 5 & 6

Clue # 4

The smaller I am made
the bigger I get.
What am I?